Beasts
Of
Immortality

Blood and Purpose

By

Paul J. Kearns

For Carrie, Quinn, and Erin.

Any mentions of members of the armed forces in this book are done so with the utmost respect to the people who have and still do serve in the military. Thank you for your service.

Content Warning:
Death, injury detail, graphic gore, torture.

Acknowledgements:

Thank you to Carrie, Quinn, and Erin for all your love and support.

Thank you to my Mum, Dad for bringing me up right, for teaching me that I can shape my own future, and teaching me to go and get what I want from life.

Thank you to Noel and Sam for the ongoing support and for believing in me.

Thank you to Louise Croft for all your help.

Thank you to all my extended family for being there when we have needed you most and for being amazing.

Thank you to all my friends, you know who you are and know I love you.

To Mr. Roberts, my former English teacher at Little lever secondary school as it was back then, thank you for being a great teacher and encouraging me to continue writing fiction.

Email Paul:
PJKauthor@hotmail.com

Other books by Paul J Kearns:
The Hunted and other Twisted Tales.
Special Operations vampire Elimination Unit

You can find Paul J Kearns on social media.
Facebook:
https://m.facebook.com/PJKearnsAuthor/
Instagram:
https://www.instagram.com/pauljkearnsauthor/
Twitter:
www.twitter.com/pjkearnsauthor

Chapter 1.

Thursday 1st December 1994.

The evening was dark and crisp with the chill of winter. Annabelle Austin walked through the streets towards her house. After work she had visited her mum and dad's house where they had made her evening meal.

She was tall with long, mousey brown hair and big, green eyes. As she walked snow began to fall. She pulled her coat up tighter around her and rubbed her belly to ward away the bitter chill of the December wind. She was now nine months pregnant and feeling every moment. Her maternity leave was set to start in three days on her due date. The soles of her feet hurt as she walked along the pavement that grew more slippery with every passing minute.

'Nearly home' she thought to herself as she was just five minutes away.

Her husband, John, would be on his way home by now. She was looking forward to seeing him after the long day she'd had.

It was seven in the evening and the streets were quiet. She could see the lights on inside the houses she passed and yearned to be out of this bitter cold.

She was startled by the sound of something cutting through the air above her. She stopped, looked up, and caught a glimpse of a large dark shadow that disappeared into the night. She felt a bit on edge but continued walking and turned down an alley that cut between two houses. A lamppost marked the midpoint, the bulb flickered as she approached. As she passed underneath it something landed behind her. She turned to see the silhouette of a huge beast stand up and fill the width of the alley. It was over eight feet tall with a large, muscular build. A row of horns that pointed out in different directions ran along each side of its head. Two limbs were folding down against its back. To Annabelle, these limbs looked like wings but she thought she must surely be mistaken. She turned frantically to run as adrenaline flooded her body sending her into a panic. The thing jumped on her and picked her up by her shoulders. It turned her around so they were facing each other. She could feel the claws of its fingers cutting into her flesh. She looked into its hard, emotionless, reptilian eyes. They glinted in the cold moonlight and looked deep into her. As if it could see into her flesh. Its hot breath rasped through its teeth and blasted in her face. The thick vile stench hit her, making her gag. It growled loudly then opened its mouth wide to expose row upon row of long, serrated teeth. It bit down into her neck and began to suck her blood. She screamed as loud as she could in an attempt to alert anyone nearby. Her vision began to spin as she felt herself losing consciousness.

'Is this how I'm going to die?' she thought. Unbeknown to her and her attacker another shadowy figure dropped into the alley. This figure moved with such grace and precision that it made no sound. Only the hiss of the blade it wielded slicing the air and cutting deep into the beast's shoulder gave away its presence. The beast roared and dropped Annabelle to the ground. With blood and saliva dripping from its mouth the beast turned to the figure and lashed out at it with a clawed hand.

The wound in Annabelle's neck throbbed. She tried to move but she had lost so much blood that her limbs felt cold and heavy. She heard the beast roar as the two figures fought. The beast threw the figure into a wall. Bricks and dust flew in all directions. Seemingly uninjured the figure stood up and leapt at the beast, slicing its chest. The beast knocked the figure aside and leapt high into the air. Annabelle heard the sound of its wings thump against the air as it flew into the cold winter's night. The figure approached Annabelle and knelt down beside her. She looked into its deep green eyes as a tiredness washed over her.

"Stay with me. You're going to be alright," the figure said in a feminine voice.

She felt it lift her shoulders and put an arm under her. Its other arm slid under her knees and she was lifted from the ground. The figure spoke to someone else close by.

"He bit her. She's alive but we need to get her to a hospital right now. She may be the one we have been waiting for." The figure spoke to her again, "Stay with me. You hear me? You're going to be…"

Annabelle's head grew heavy and she slipped into the comfortable dark of unconsciousness.

Chapter 2.

Annabelle drifted in and out of consciousness. Voices barked orders as she was rushed down corridors. The rhythmic beep of a heart monitor drifted through Annabelle's nightmares of monsters, teeth, blood, and being bitten. The dream began to fade but the sounds remained and grew louder. As she opened her eyes she found she was looking at a ceiling she didn't recognise. She turned her head to the left and saw a long green and white hospital ward. Nurses walked among beds with patients lay in them. Each patient had wires and tubes coming from them that were attached to machines and equipment that beeped and pinged. Through the cacophony of noise and unfamiliar voices, she heard one of them say her name.

"Annabelle…Mrs. Austin. Can you hear me?"
She turned her head to the right and saw that a tall Asian man was looking down at her. He had a kind smile and a stethoscope hung around his neck.

"Mrs. Austin, I see you're awake. I'm Doctor Khan. Do you know where you are?" he said.

"No. I…um…I…" She murmured.

"You're in Manchester Royal Infirmary. You were injured in a violent attack two days ago. Do you remember that?" he said.

"Er… I remember…er… I remember walking home from my mum and dad's… and waking up here, just now," she said.

She moved her head and noticed the dressing on her neck. If she hadn't been sedated she would have panicked and been hysterical. The best she could muster was a lethargic question.

"What happened? What happened to me?" she mumbled.

"There is a police inspector who wants to talk to you. He wants to know who brought you here. You have lost a third of your total blood volume through a wound in your neck. Amazingly though the wound had already started to heal when you were brought in. The inspector wants to speak to you as soon as you're able. Just let a member of staff or me know as soon as you're ready," he said.

"I really don't remember anything doctor. I've only just woken up," she said.

"Ok, Mrs. Austin, don't worry. If you do remember anything just let one of the nurses know and they'll let the inspector know," he said.
He smiled then turned to walk away.

"Doctor," said Annabelle as she clasped his arm.
He turned back to her and saw she had a worried expression on her face.

"My babies?" she said in a soft voice.

"They're both well and doing fine. We performed an ultrasound after we stabilised you," he said with a reassuring smile.

"Thank you," she said and smiled back at him.
She lay her head back down on the pillow and relaxed.

"Try to get up and eat something. You need to build your strength," he said.
Annabelle closed her eyes. As she began to fall asleep a nurse pulled the curtain around her bed. John came in and helped her up out of bed. They walked outside and got in his car. As they drove home John sat in silence.

"Are you ok?" Annabelle said.

John turned to look at her but remained silent.

"When did you hear that I was in hospital?" she said.
But John remained silent.

"John, what's wrong?" she said.
But he still sat in silence.

"Why won't you talk to me?" she said.
As she spoke the last sentence his mouth dropped open and the long fingers of a hand reached out over his tongue and wrapped down over his lower lip and chin. The hand forced his jaw to open as far as it could and then kept going. The corners of his mouth began to split exposing the muscle as blood ran down his cheeks. Something dark moved at the back of his throat. As she looked at it she realiscd it was the lips of another mouth. They parted to reveal long serrated teeth and a low roar bellowed from inside. Annabelle sat up in her hospital bed and screamed. A nurse opened the curtain and looked in.

"Are you ok?" he said.

"Yes, sorry. I was just having a bad dream," said Annabelle.
A tall, fast moving shadow fell across the curtain. The nurse was lifted off the floor and he screamed as blood splattered across the curtain.
Annabelle sat up in her bed and screamed. A nurse stood next to her jumped.

"Oh my! Are you ok, Mrs. Austin," she said.

"Yes, sorry. I keep having bad dreams," said Annabelle.

"You've been through a lot. A couple of days rest and you will start to feel better. I have some food for you.

Dr. Khan says you need to eat," said the nurse.

"Oh, yes please. I'm so hungry," said Annabelle as she sat up.

An hour later she was starting to feel better as Dr. Khan came to check up on her.

"Are you ready to talk to the police about the attack?" he said.

"No, I'm sorry, I'm still not ready. I feel better but I still can't remember anything," she said.

"That's ok. There is no rush," he said.

Annabelle's Mum and Dad and her husband, John, came to visit her the next morning. Sue and Michael stood on one side of her bed and John stood on the other. Her parents hugged her and as they did they all began to cry.

"Oh my God, I'm so glad you're ok. I was so scared when the police came to our house," said Sue as tears ran down her face.

"I was scared too. I woke up here and I didn't know where I was. I'm so happy to see you," she said.
John sat down on the edge of the bed and held her hand.

"I'm so happy you're getting better. Your work friends rang to say that they hope you're ok and get well soon. Your boss said you can start your maternity leave now, then take all the time you need," said John.
He leaned in and kissed her. "I was so worried for you and our babies. I love you so much."
She could see the tears as they welled in his eyes and she kissed him.

"I love you too," she said.

Doctor Khan came onto the ward and talked to the four of them.

"Hello. How are you all?" he said.

"We're happy to see her awake and getting better. Thank you for all you have done," said John.

"You're very welcome. She is doing well. She still doesn't know who brought her in, but that's ok. Some memory loss is expected in cases like this. The staff in A&E said that it was a tall person dressed entirely in black from head to toe. They banged on the door and then sped away in a black van. Do you know who that might have been?" said Dr. Khan

"No, I have no idea," said John.

"I can't think of anyone who that might be either," said Michael.

"Whoever it was they saved your life and the babies' lives too. You had lost so much blood I seriously didn't think you would survive. We gave you blood transfusions, treated your wounds, and performed an ultrasound. You'll be pleased to know that all the tests we have done show you are on the mend and the babies are both doing fine. You still need to rest and we'll keep you on pain relief. We want to keep you in for observation, if everything is going ok you can go home in the next two days," said Dr. Khan.

"You hear that, love. That's great thank you doc…I mean doctor," said John.

"You are all welcome. I'll leave you to enjoy the rest of your visiting time together now. See you later," said Dr. Khan.

When visiting hours were over the family said their tearful goodbyes but they assured Annabelle they would be back the next morning.

Later that day Annabelle was moved to her own room. She woke in the night to find she was in her own bed at home. She reached over onto John's side but he wasn't there. A hand grabbed her wrist then dragged her off the bed and onto the floor. The beast from the night she was attacked bit deep into her neck. She tasted blood and felt a tearing pain in her stomach. A child's screams filled her mind and the pain in her stomach forced her to wake up for real. As she did she realised the pain was real too and it became unbearable. She clenched her teeth together and let out a stifled scream. She threw off the sheets from on the bed and through her nightgown she could see a large shape on her abdomen. She had the urge to cough and when she did blood poured out of her mouth. She began to cry and scream as she dabbed her fingers at the blood around her mouth. She slammed her palm against the alarm button and a nurse walked into her room. The sight she saw before her made her scream too. She picked up the nearest wall mounted phone and called for assistance. In moments a team of doctors and nurses came running into the room with a trolley full of equipment. Annabelle was rushed into surgery and when her nightdress was removed the team gasped. The large protrusion in Annabelle's abdomen was the shape of a child's foot.

There was a flurry of activity as the nurses prepped her for surgery and soon the surgeons, Dr. Baker and Dr. Fitzgerald, began to operate. They opened up her abdomen and found one of the baby's feet had burst through the placenta, the womb, had torn her intestines, and had almost pushed through the muscle wall. They performed an emergency caesarean section and the first baby was delivered. He was six pounds and four ounces, 46cm long and despite the complications was a healthy boy.

The baby whose foot had done the damage was delivered. Dr. Baker put her hands in Annabelle's stomach and began to lift him out.

"Oh my god. I'm going to need some help here," she said.

Across town John, Michael and Sue were driving to the hospital as fast as they could. The hospital had contacted them and told them Annabelle was having complications and she had been rushed into surgery. They arrived at the hospital and rushed to the ward Annabelle had been staying on. A nurse escorted them to the waiting room just down the corridor from the operating theatre. The room was long and rectangular with a row of chairs on both sides. There was a table full of magazines in the middle of the room but John, Michael and Sue couldn't even bring themselves to look at them. Through the doors down the corridor, they heard the cries of a baby.

Dr. Baker and one of the nurses lifted the baby onto a small table next to the operating table Annabelle lay on and cleaned him up. He was huge, weighing 25 pounds, 71 cm in length and his skin was completely white; he was also not breathing. Dr. Baker held him up by his ankles and the nurse slapped his bottom. He took a deep breath and cried out an otherworldly screech.

Dr. Fitzgerald had just finished repairing Annabelle's intestines when she stopped breathing and her heartbeat dropped dramatically. The surgeons resuscitated her. They got her heart stabilised but her lungs were not responding. They connected her to a ventilator and tried to get her to breathe for herself again for half an hour. They still hadn't sewn her stomach closed when her heart stopped again. They defibrillated her heart five times without success. Dr. Baker lowered her head, when she raised it again she had tears in her eyes.

"Mrs. Annabelle Austin. Time of death, 3.37 am on the 4th December, 1994," she said.
One of the nurses wrote it down in the surgery notes. Dr. Baker took off her latex gloves, her mask, and her surgical overalls. She walked into the washroom cleaned herself up with anti-bacterial soap and prepared herself to inform Annabelle's family. She didn't have much experience in breaking bad news to the patient's family. This would be only the third time in her twenty year career, but she knew that it had to be done. Despite being the worst part of the job it was only fair on the family.

She walked through the door to where they sat in the waiting room. They were all huddled together on one row of chairs. John stood up as she walked towards them. He was twenty seven years old. His brown hair was a mess after he had tried to sleep but had not been able to settle. From the red line around his eyes it was obvious that he had been crying.

Michael and Sue looked up at her too. Michael's hair was grey and he looked older than his years due to a life working down a coal mine and later in construction. Sue looked like an older version of Annabelle. The lids of her blue eyes were red and the tracks of her tears were still present on her face.

"How is, Annabelle?" said John in little more than a whisper.

Dr. Baker took a deep breath.

"We did everything we could. I am so sorry. She passed away just a few minutes ago. We tried to revive her for over half an hour. There is just nothing more we could do," she said.

Sue began to sob and Michael wrapped his arms around her and held her close. His bottom lip trembled, then big silent tears rolled down his face. John put his head down, then stumbled a little, Dr. Baker caught him by the arm and helped him to sit down. When he raised his head his face was racked with pain and the tears flowed openly down his face.

"The Babies. My…my sons?" John managed to say.

"They're both doing fine. They were successfully delivered before Annabelle developed further complications," said Dr. Baker.

She wanted to try and force a smile but found that she couldn't.

"What happened? We saw her this morning and she was fine," said John.

His voice trembled uncontrollably.

"Annabelle's womb and intestines were ruptured which caused blood poisoning. We performed a caesarean section and began to repair her intestines. At that point Annabelle stopped breathing. We resuscitated her but she went into cardiac arrest, we tried repeatedly to restart her heart but there was nothing else we could do. I honestly am so sorry," she said.

She couldn't keep her voice from trembling.

John put his head down and cried. Dr. Baker put her hand on his shoulder to comfort him as he lifted his head.

"We did all we could," said Dr. Baker.

"We-We know. I just can't believe it. Can we see her?" he said.

"We just need a few more minutes then you can go and say goodbye," she said.

"Can I see my children?" he said.

"Yes. Do you know that one of your twins has abnormalities?" said Dr. Baker.

"Abnormalities? No, I had no idea. Last time we had a scan they said everything was fine. What do you mean by abnormalities?" said John as his voice quivered.

"I think you all should follow me," said Dr. Baker. She led them through to a room with two incubators next to each other. Nurses rushed around them doing tests and Dr. Baker took John, Michael and Sue over to them. John looked in at the big white baby. He looked normal just very big for a newborn.

"I thought you said he had abnormalities?" said John.

"Well, he weighs twenty five pounds and he's seventy-one centimeters. For a new born he would be consider abnormal," said Dr. Baker.

"What has caused this?" said John.

"We're not sure yet. It could be a variety of different things. He might have some form of gigantism and albinism. There might be other complications though. His internal organs might not be able to function properly, or in a worst case scenario, they could fail. That is all speculation at this point though until we can run more tests. Are you sure the scans didn't show any of this?" she said.

"Yes, we had a scan about a month ago and Dr. Khan said there was a scan done when they brought Annabelle in. He said everything was o-o-ok," John said as he stumbled over his words and two tears rolled down his face.

"I'm sorry John, I don't mean to upset you. Wait here I just need to speak to Dr. Khan," said Dr. Baker.

She walked out of the room. John looked at his babies and the large baby looked back at him. His big yellowish-green eyes focused on his dad's face and he smiled. John tried to smile back but it felt like his heart was going to tear itself in two. He walked over to the other incubator and the baby looked tiny in comparison. He was bright red with his eyes shut tight and lay completely still. Only his little chest rose and fell as he breathed.

Dr. Baker walked into the corridor just outside the room. She picked up the closest wall-mounted phone and keyed in the number for the staff sleeping room. The groggy voice of a man answered,

"Hello?"

"Is Dr. Harmeen Khan in one of the bunks?" she said.

"Yes, hold on," said the man.

A few seconds later Dr. Khan answered the phone.

"Hello," he said drowsily.

"Hello, Harmeen, it's Dr. Baker. I've just come from performing surgery on Annabelle Austin. She was rushed into surgery this morning."

"Ah, Hello Dr. Baker. Yes, I Heard. How is she?" Said Dr. Khan.

"Unfortunately, she…er, she died in surgery," she said.

"My god. How? Have her family been informed?" he said.

Dr. Baker explained how Annabelle had died.

"Her Mum and dad and husband are here. They're with the babies now. That is the reason I rang you. One of the babies has abnormalities that have caused him to be overly large. Mr. Austin says he knew nothing of this. He said that you had a scan done and it came back all clear."

"Yes…er, yes. The scan was clear. There was no indication of any abnormalities," said Dr. Khan.

"Are you sure?" said Dr. Baker.

"Yes. I examined the results. They were all clear," said Dr. Khan.

"I'm sorry to pull you from your break but I think you better come and see for yourself. Could you bring the scan results with you too please?" said Dr. Baker.

"Yes, of course. I'll be there in ten minutes," said Dr. Khan.

Chapter 3.

"My god," said Dr. Khan as he looked at the big white baby. "You're sure this is one of Mrs. Austin's babies?"

"Dr. Khan, I delivered these babies myself," said Dr. Baker.

"I know, I'm sorry. I didn't mean to question your judgement. It's just, well, we did a scan and everything was ok. There were no signs of deformity or any kind of anomalies. It's just so strange. How can a child develop such abnormalities in such a small space of time?" said Dr. Khan.

"They don't. I've never seen anything like this. We'll have to keep him in for assessment," said Dr. Baker.

"I'll get him moved onto the postnatal ward. We can keep him under constant observation there," said Dr. Khan.

"That's a good idea," said Dr. Baker.
Dr. Khan walked over to John, Michael and Sue and explained everything he and Dr. Baker had discussed.

"We just need to keep him in and see how the next few days play out," he said.

"What's wrong with him?" said John.

"It's too early to say. This is all a shock to us all. I know this might be a bad time but have you thought of names for the children. It will just be easier to fill in their birth records if we have names for the children," said Dr. Khan.

"Annabelle wants..." John's voice trembled and he closed his eyes. Sue put a hand on his shoulder and when his opened his eyes he said. "Annabelle wanted to name them Vincent Andrew after my grandads and Alexander

Peter after her grandads."

"Good strong names," said Michael.

"What about Annabelle?" Sue said, her voice was quiet and soft.

"Her body will be released in a few days. You should know, before we do, the police may want to examine her," said Dr. Khan.

"Can we see her? I need to see my girl just one last time. I need to say goodbye," said Sue.

"Of course, please follow me," said Dr. Khan. He quietly led them from the room and through a door that led to a private room where Annabelle's body lay on a bed. She was covered up to her neck with a white sheet. Sue began to weep when she saw her.

"My baby, oh my baby. She looks just like she's sleeping."
She tried to regain her composure but tears still ran down her face. She held Michael's hand as they walked over to her daughter's body. Sue stroked her hair and spoke to her in a whisper.

"I love you, I always have. Even since the first moment I found out I was pregnant with you. When I gave birth to you the nurse passed you to me all wrapped in a towel. You were the most beautiful thing I had ever seen. You still are the most beautiful thing I have ever seen. I love you so much."

Michael's shoulders shook as he silently wept.

"I love you, my little girl. I wish I could have been there to save you. I'm going to miss you," he said.

John walked over, put his arm around Michael's shoulder and gave him a squeeze. He then knelt down next to Sue and took hold of Annabelle's hand. He spoke to her and tears rolled down his face.

"I can't believe I've lost you, I thought we were going to spend the rest of our lives together. I'm sorry I wasn't there to protect you. I wish I could have been. I love you, always have…always will. I don't know what I'll do without you. It was never meant to be like this. I thought we would watch the kids grow. Have holidays, Christmases, and birthdays together. I'll…I'll raise the boys to know your name. They will know how beautiful their mum was. What an amazing person you were. I love you Annabelle Austin."

He kissed her cheek, then stood up and turned away but he was suddenly unsteady on his feet. His legs gave way and he fell to his knees where he let out an anguished wail. Sue and Michael gathered him up and pulled him to them. They all hugged and cried together.

The next few days were some of the hardest of John's life. His parents had died when he was a child and his grandmother, who had raised him, had died two years ago. Annabelle had been the love of his life and now her parents and the twins were all he had. The hospital let him stay in a relative's room for the next three days while they did tests on Vincent.

Two days after the twins were born Dr. Khan walked onto the ward in which they were being cared for. The nurse on duty approached him.

"Hello Dr. Khan," she said.

"Good morning, Nurse Jarvis. How are the twins?" he said and flashed his kind smile.

"Alex is good, he is taking between five and 10 ml per feed. He has filled his nappy twice since last night.

Vincent on the other hand has refused to take any milk. Every time we have tried to feed him he cries. We have changed his nappies too but he hasn't produced anything," she said.

"He completely refuses food? That's odd. Does he even cry to be fed?" he said.

"No doctor, he doesn't usually cry at all. He only cries when we try to feed him milk. In the end we give up because he became hysterical. We were scared he would injure himself. He's strong too, I've never known a baby to possess such strength," she said.

"I see. Is there anything else I should know?" said Dr. Khan as he frowned in confusion.

"Yes. We opened the curtains yesterday. As soon as the sunlight touched his skin he began screaming as if it was hurting him. Tiny blisters started to form everywhere that the light touched. We closed the curtains and his skin returned to normal in an instant. We have logged it all in his medical records. Do you have any idea what that could be, Doctor?" she said,

"That is strange. I have heard of conditions that cause extreme photosensitivity but none where the patient's skin heals instantly. I'll have to look into it. It looks like we'll have to keep him in for a few more days," he said.

"Ok, thank you, doctor," she said.

"Thank you, nurse Jarvis. I'll inform his father," he said.

Chapter 4.

Annabelle's funeral took place on 19th December at the St Paul Church in Salford. The atmosphere was understandably sombre. John, Michael and Sue turned up early and greeted all her family and friends as they came into the church. They all took their seats and the priest began the service.

"We are gathered here today to celebrate the life of Annabelle Austin…"
He continued to talk for fifteen minutes and then invited the mourners to join him in saying a prayer that Michael had prepared. Annabelle's friend, Sophie, then took to the microphone and read a poem she had written for her friend. She was composed but tears ran down her face as she read. When she finished she returned to her seat. John stood up and went to the microphone.

"When Annabelle and I went on our first date I was incredibly nervous. I had met her before through our mutual friends Tom and Sophie. They had set us up on a date after I had asked Tom about her. I thought she was gorgeous, she always will be gorgeous to me. The first time I met her I had made a fool of myself so I wasn't expecting her to meet me for the date. She did though and perfectly on time too; just like she said she would. We went to a little Italian restaurant. She had a way of making people feel at ease. My nervousness disappeared as we laughed, talked, and got to know each other. It was wonderful, she was wonderful. We sat and talked for so long that in the end the owners had to ask us to leave because they wanted to close up and go home. We talked on the phone every night in the week that followed and arranged a second date; then a third. That was five years ago. We only got married at the beginning of last year. I thought we would be together until we were old. This world gives but it takes so much as payment. The boys are gorgeous just like you, Annabelle. I'll raise them to remember you as though you were still here. When my grandma died you told me 'If we live in the hearts of those we leave behind we never really die.' You will never die, Anna Austin, because you will always be in my heart and the hearts of our children."

He then recited one of Annabelle's favourite poems. He struggled and his voice trembled as he read but eventually he finished reading.

'Wild Horses' by The Rolling Stones was played as the pallbearers carried her coffin outside to the hearse. She was then buried at Agecroft cemetery.

Everyone shed a lot of tears as they lowered her coffin into the ground. They all stood around and watched as the priest said a final prayer. No one noticed the tall woman in the black hooded cloak who stood well away from the crowd. As John threw a single rose onto Annabelle's coffin she swept her long blonde hair away from her face. Tears ran down her purple, scaled skin and she wiped them away from her deep green, reptilian eyes. No one at the funeral knew who she was and she was not part of the group, but like them she was saddened by Annabelle's death. She had waited a long time for someone like Annabelle.

Chapter 5.

After the night he had attacked Annabelle the vampire, Lord Ruhsarr, returned to his hideout deep in the Himalayan Mountains. For four long days he paced back and forth across the polished floors of the great hall carved deep into the heart of one of the mountains. He could see perfectly in the sparsely lit cavernous room. The small amount of light there was reflected off the horns that ran from the corners of his eyes, along both sides of his head and up to the crown of his skull. It shimmered off his dark green scales that covered the entirety of his body. Around his face they were small but over his limbs and torso they were larger and covered in thorns. He stretched out his long dragon-like wings, gave them a little shake and then folded them down over his back again. He hadn't fed in the passing days and he had little need for sleep.

One of his officers approached him. He was a short well-built vampire by the name of Drake. In his human life he had been an Italian soldier. Now he was a high ranking officer in Ruhsarr's army.

"Good evening, Sir. Please tell me if I am interrupting your train of thought, but you have been pacing for four consecutive days now," said Drake.

"Four days? I didn't realise it had been that long," said Ruhsarr.

"Yes sir, it has been that long. I was wondering if you need to consult with someone. A problem shared is a problem halved. It would be an honour if you would allow me to help you, my Lord," said Drake.

"My problems, Drake, are beyond your understanding

and above your authority," said Ruhsarr.

"Please, have some faith in me, sir. I want to help in any way I can," said Drake in a friendly tone.

Ruhsarr fixed him with a glare and a raised eyebrow. This expression would have chilled most to the bone but Drake just stood with a pleasant smile on his face and Ruhsarr's glare softened.

"Ok. Ok, I may have made a… mistake," said Ruhsarr.

"A, mistake, sir? How could one as mighty as you have made a mistake?" said Drake.

"I cannot remember asking for, nor do I need, you to massage my ego, Drake," said Ruhsarr with a growl.

"No sir. I apologise," said Drake with a bow of his head. "What mistake did you make sir?"

"Well, I, er, I like to go out and feed in different places. I went to the Northwest of England and I selected a woman. Her blood was sweet and her flesh tender," said Ruhsarr.

"Sounds like a pleasant meal," said Drake.

"She was also pregnant," said Ruhsarr.

"She was pregnant?!" said Drake, his eyes wide with a deep seated fear.

"I was hungry and she was the first person I came across," said Ruhsarr.

"Please, sir. Please tell me you killed her!" said Drake.

"I feed on pregnant women all the time. It has never been a problem before. I did try to drain her but I was...interrupted," said Ruhsarr.

"You feed on pregnant women!? You were interrupted!? Sir, did you forget about the dragon's curse?" said Drake.

"The curse! The curse! That is all you people ever say.

I am Ruhsarr Miehyelzah and I will not be bound by the final words of a long dead dragon!"

"Ok, sir. I apologise. Who interrupted you?" said Drake.

"That S.O.V.E.U. That bitch, Andra, attacked me. She tried to cut off my wings, so I flew away to have a chance to heal. I hoped she would try and follow me. Instead, she picked up the woman, put her in a van and they took her to a hospital. There was no way I could have got to her without revealing myself and our kind," said Ruhsarr.

"What happened to this…woman?" said Drake.

"I have a spy in the hospital. They told me the woman gave birth to a pair of twins right before she died. Unfortunately, the babies survived. From the information they gave me they assume that one is human and one is a vampire," said Ruhsarr.

Drake's eyes were wide with terror. In horror and rage he chastised Ruhsarr,
"What have you done to us?! What have you done? This is the end! You, our Lord, our protector, have brought the end of our race upon all of us! You are an imbecile! An insolent fool!"

Ruhsarr clamped his hand around Drake's throat and lifted him off the ground before he had chance to say another word.

"Who do you think you are talking to?" growled Ruhsarr.

Drake gasped for breath as he fought against the hand squeezing his neck. It was no use, Ruhsarr was far too strong for him to fight off.

"You dare to reprimand me? You seem to have

forgotten your place, Drake!" he thought for a moment and then continued. "Seeing as you are so upset that I have 'brought the end of our race upon us all' as you put it, I have a job for you. Find these children, I want them dead; all their family too. The main target is the human child. It is imperative that he dies."

He opened his hand and Drake fell clumsily to the floor. His throat screamed as his lungs drew in as much air they could.

"How my Lord?" croaked Drake.

"Butcher him. Tear him apart. Make him suffer," said Ruhsarr with a grin.

"Yes, my Lord. Your wish is my command, my Lord," said Drake.

"Now go. Gather your best soldiers and do not return until you have fulfilled this mission," said Ruhsarr. With that Drake bowed and left Ruhsarr. He rounded up a handful of soldiers, they gathered their equipment and left for England.

Incidents of this nature do not stay secret for long. There were whispers of the boy's existence, then rumours, and before long news of twins spread throughout the vampire empire.

Chapter 6.

Late March 1995

The three months that followed Annabelle's funeral passed slowly and painfully for John. He found himself crying at all times of the day and night but knew he had to get his life back together. He had no choice, he had two young children to look after now. Fortunately, Michael and Sue were on hand and would help with the children whenever they had a chance.

It was 9 pm. The nights were getting lighter and there was a hint of warmth in those early spring days. Vincent and Alex were upstairs in bed. Downstairs the adults were sat in the living room.

"Do you want a beer?" said John.

"Yes please," said Michael.

"Erm, he means no thank you," said Sue.

"Come on. I can have one," said Michael.

"Yea, come on Sue. Let him have at least one," said John with a smile.

Sue looked at John with a fake scowl on her face, then smiled.

"Ok. Just the one. Remember though, Doctor Morris said you need to watch your weight," she said.

"You know Sue is probably right. You better just have a coffee," said John with a grin.

"Less of the yap, you. Pass the beer," said Michael. John laughed as he popped the cap off a bottle and passed it to him. Sue poured herself a small glass of wine and they all settled down to watch some evening T.V. shows.

Something heavy and wet hit the kitchen window at the back of the house and made them all jump. They all ran into the kitchen and to their shock, they saw blood splattered all over the large rear window. Michael summoned up the courage to unlock the back door and step out into the cool night.

"Hello? I know you are out here," he said.

He looked around the garden and as his eyes adjusted to the darkness he saw the silhouette of a tall man.

"Did you do this? What the fuck is this all about, eh? Go on piss off and annoy someone else," he said.

"Who's out there Michael?" said Sue.

John ran outside and stood next to Michael.

"Who are you? What hell are you doing here?" said John.

The man took two slow steps towards them.

"Stay there!" said Michael and John in unison.

Before they finished the sentence he was stood right infront of them. This close up they could see how pale his face was. He let out a snarl then with inhuman speed lifted John up by his neck then threw him. He crashed through the kitchen window and landed on the floor. His clothes and skin were shredded by the glass. Sue ran over to him as the man walked into the house holding Michael up by the throat.

"Oh, God. Michael!" said Sue.

"Where are the children?" said Drake.

Sue shook her head and cried. Drake placed his other hand on Michael's shoulder and clenched it into a fist. Michael's bones cracked and he cried out in pain.

"Tell me where the children are!" said Drake with more force.

"We're not going to tell you, you piece of shit," said Michael, his voice hoarse from the pressure.

Drake tightened the grip around Michael's throat and his fingers dug into the flesh. Michael spluttered and choked as his oesophagus and Trachea closed. Blood started to pour from his mouth. With a jerk of his arm Drake crushed Michael's neck. Sue screamed and staggered back; shaking her head in denial. Drake flashed an evil smile at her as he dropped Michael's twitching body to the floor. She barely had time to blink before he grabbed her by the back of her blouse collar and spun her around so they were face to face.

"Where are the children?!" he said spraying her face with spittle.
Sue sobbed and raked at his hand with her nails but it was no use.

"Don't tell him," said John as he used the kitchen worktop to pull himself up from the floor.

"You remind me of my mother," Drake said softly to Sue. "Do you know the last thing my mother said to me before she died?"

"No," said Sue in a barely audible whisper.

"Nothing, she just screamed as I bit out her throat," he said in an ominous tone.

His grip had loosened and Sue tried to run. In a flash he grabbed her head, twisted it, and broke her neck. He swung her limp body and threw her at the wall. John's rage finally outweighed his fear. He grabbed a wooden chair and smashed it against Drake's back. Splinters of wood cascaded in all directions. Without flinching Drake turned, grabbed John by the throat, leapt across the room and slammed him into the wall. John cried out in pain as his ribs cracked but the position of Drake's hand kept his jaw clamped shut. He looked at John and smiled at the fear he saw in his eyes. John saw only a sadistic glint of pleasure in the eyes of this thing that he realised was not human. The man opened his mouth so wide his chin touched his neck. His teeth grew long and serrated. His eyes turned purple and he let out a roar that made John's ears bleed. A noise began to drift through the house, quiet at first but it quickly got louder. It was the noise Drake wanted to hear, the cries of two children.

"I knew they would be upstairs. You humans always keep your young upstairs. You seem to think they'll be safe up there," he laughed. "How have you found looking after a vampire? I must say, I'm impressed, not many humans could. It's almost a shame you have to die,"

He opened his mouth again but stopped abruptly and his lips quivered. Blood rose up inside his throat then poured from his mouth and his eyes squinted in pain. He and John looked down at the same time. Three inches of a silver blade protruded from the centre of Drake's chest. It twisted ninety degrees of its own volition. In a last ditch attempt Drake tried to bite John but less than an inch away from his neck, Drake's face turned grey. He dropped John and seemed uneasy on his feet just before his knees disintegrated. He fell to the floor and shattered into a cloud of ash and embers.

Between coughs John could see a tall woman stood where the man had been. She was six and a half feet tall and dressed head to toe in a close fitting, black material. To John, she looked like a ninja. The material covered her entire body except for her deep green eyes. The skin around her eyes was light purple and covered in small scales. In her hands she held a staff with a short blade on one end and a crescent moon shaped blade on the other. Both of which were covered in ash. John pressed himself back to the wall. His mouth hung open and his eyes were wide with terror. She reached up to her face and pulled away the material.

"You don't need to be afraid of me, John," she said.

"Who... who the hell are you? What the fuck was he? Oh my god! Oh my god! Michael, Sue. We need to call the police," he said his voice fraught with panic.

She grabbed him and picked him up under his arms and looked him right in the eyes.

"I need you calm right now. I know this is crazy but I need you to focus," she said.

"Calm? Calm? How the fuck I'm I supposed to be calm. I've just seen a fucking, whatever the fuck he was, kill my in-laws, and now I'm talking to a purple...ninja...lizard lady, and you want me to calm down?!" He said hysterically.

"Calm down!" she said as she put him down then grabbed him by the face "I need you calm right now. We haven't got time for this bullshit. I'm sorry about your in-laws, really I am but we need to get your children out of here right now. There are more men like him on their way. They want to kill your children and you. If I hadn't got here in time he would have succeeded. So pull yourself together and let's go. I have a van outside. We need to go right now," she said.

"Ok...ok. The twins are upstairs," said John quickly.

They ran upstairs and John handed the woman a bag. She filled it with clothes while he filled another with nappies, wipes, feeding bottles, formula milk, and dummies. They got the babies out of their cots, ran down the stairs, out the back door and through the garden to the back street. All around there were piles of ash and clothes. In the alley there was a black car with the windscreen smashed in and ash covered the driver's seat. Just infront of it stood a black, high roofed Ford Transit van. The side door slid open. Inside were four soldiers dressed in black Kevlar body armour, helmets, and black balaclavas. The one who opened the door motioned with a hand for them to get in. John was a bit hesitant but climbed in closely followed by the woman.

A black BMW 5 series skidded into the far end of the back street. The van set off as the soldier slid the door shut. The two soldiers in the back slid open metal panels in the back doors, pointed their M16s out and began shooting at the car as both vehicles sped down the alley and skidded onto the street. As they did a Volvo joined the chase. John could hear the clatter of bullets hitting the back of the van.

"Don't worry. The armour on this vehicle is too thick for their bullets," said the woman.

The three vehicles sped through the streets exchanging gunfire until a burst of bullets tore through the skull of the driver of the BMW. His brains splattered but were already turning to ash as they landed on the passengers. The car swerved then slammed into another vehicle parked on the side of the road, flipped and burst into flames. The three other burning vampires tore themselves from the wreck before they exploded into lumps of ash. The Volvo continued to chase the van as it sped up a slip road on to a duel carriageway.

"What the hell is going on?" John shouted to be heard over the engines and gunfire. "Tell me right now!"

"The people chasing us are vampires and they want to kill your babies. Especially the little one," said the woman.

" What the hell do you mean, vampires? Why would they want to kill babies?" said John.

"According to an ancient prophecy the first of their kind, Ruhsarr, was cursed. The prophecy tells of two brothers born to a mother who survives an attack by Ruhsarr. One brother will be a vampire and the other a human. The human child will rise up and destroy the vampire race. Ruhsarr is the one who attacked Annabelle. Your babies are those brothers!"
The Volvo slammed into the side of the van they all stumbled.

"What do you mean vampires? Why do you keep saying that?" John said.

"Vampires, creatures of the night, but these aren't some un-dead, ethereal entities who have to be invited across a threshold and can't cross bodies of water. They're fast, vicious, and extremely powerful. They are also militarised. An army created and trained by their dark Lord, Ruhsarr," said the woman.

"But vampires aren't real," said John.

"They're as real as you and me. Their hearts beat, they have reflections and they cast shadows. They're flesh and blood. Take a look outside if you don't believe me. They're shooting at us right now. We could pull over and you can have a chat with them if you like," she replied.

"They're trying to get infront of us," shouted the

driver.

"Use the side panel," Shouted the woman.

One of the soldiers pulled open the panel and shot into the car. Bullets rattled all over the van in retaliation. The car rammed them again and the soldier fell back into the van.

"Stay down and stay back," the woman shouted to John.

He shuffled back and the soldier who had fallen gave him a Kevlar jacket.

"Cover the kids," he said.

John placed it over the twins and got as low to the floor as he could.

The woman opened a large lockbox that was welded to the chassis of the van and took out a multiple grenade launcher. She stepped towards the side door and slid it wide open. John watched as bullets tore her clothing and flesh but she just stood there and took the hits without so much as a flinch. She pointed the grenade launcher into the back window of the Volvo and squeezed the trigger. There was a pop of compressed air and a canister flew into the back of the car. It bounced around the interior before coming to rest on the rear seat between two of the vampires. With a hiss it began to emit a silver gas. The vampires started to cough, then scream and claw at their flesh. Their skin disintegrated like smouldering paper and dissolved right through to the muscles. Soon their flesh was eaten right down to the bones. The car swerved and slammed into the central reservation and sent smouldering bones clattering against the windscreen.

"Man, I fucking love this stuff!" she said as she slid the door shut.

"Tear gas kills them?" said John.

"It's not just tear gas. Its CS gas infused with powdered silver. It's poisonous to humans in large quantities but to vampires, just a tiny amount is enough to make them burn like paper dolls," she said with a grin and knelt down next to him. He saw that her flesh had healed where the bullets had hit, leaving patches of purple, scaled, skin showing through her clothes.

"How do you do that?" said John.

"What?" she said.

"Get shot like that and then heal in seconds," he said.

"Unfortunately Ruhsarr made me too. Fortunately, I'm not a vampire," she said.

"What are you?" he said.

"I don't think anyone has come up with a name for what I am. As far as I know I'm the only one of my kind. So…a dragon lady, maybe. All I can tell you is I'm very old," she said.

"What have dragons got to do with vampires?" he said.

"Ruhsarr became the first vampire after he was bitten by a dragon. All that stuff about bats is Hollywood bullshit," she said.

"How old are you?" he said.

"I am older than any person who has ever lived. There are a few vampires who were made around the same time as me, but that is all you need to know; for now anyway," she said.

"Just the one thing?" he said.

"Go on?" she said.

"What's your name?" he said.

"I'm Andra Hudson. These guys and the rest of our crew are the S.O.V.E.U," she said with a smile.

There was an explosion behind the van that flipped the car through the air.

"I fucking hate vampires," said one of the soldiers at the back.

The car landed on its roof in a crumpled wreck and the van pulled off the dual carriageway. They drove through the streets of Salford and then pulled into the entrance of a rusty, old, corrugated iron warehouse with a sign that read Jones Distribution. As they drove towards the building a huge door slid open, then immediately slid shut behind them once they were inside.

Chapter 7.

The warehouse was half the size of a football pitch. It was a forty foot high, steel-alloy internal framework with an outer layer of corrugated steel. The rust was merely an extremely convincing paint job which made it completely inconspicuous. It looked like any other warehouse.

On the inside the ground floor was set out as a standard warehouse. Down the centre there was an aisle wide enough to drive a forklift truck and on either side there were industrial shelving filled with crates. Towards the back were a few offices, a cafeteria, and toilets.

The van drove down the central aisle and stopped. There was a mechanical whine as the floor of the aisle infront of them lowered to form a ramp. The van drove down into the first of nine subterranean levels and the ramp raised back up to form the aisle again.

On these lower levels were science labs, engineering workshops, gyms, physical training courses, shooting ranges, sleeping quarters, and kitchens. This was all fortified with six inches of steel and three feet of reinforced concrete. The place was a fortress.

The driver eased on the brakes and parked in a space between two other similar vans. Andra slid the door open and stepped out, closely followed by John.

"Where are we?" he said.

"At this current moment you are in Base 115 of the S.O.V.E.U. You are one of only a small proportion of non-military personnel to ever see the lower levels of this base. You can never tell anyone anything you see or hear within these walls. Do you understand?" said

Andra.

"Yes I understand I'm just wondering why you brought me here?" said John.

"This one of the most secure military bases in the country. The vampires are looking for you but they don't know this place exists. You are welcome to stay here indefinitely," she said.

"Indefinitely? But what about my in-laws? What about my job?" he said.

"You don't have to worry about your job anymore. Your days of working as a car mechanic are over. You are now solely the protector of your children. Anything you need shall be provided. The situation surrounding your In-laws is more difficult but I can sort things out so it looks like their deaths were the result of a robbery gone wrong. It's not going to be easy but it's not impossible," she said.

"How can you be so flippant? My In-laws are dead. There's going to need to be a murder investigation and funerals. We need to call the police these people need to be caught," he said.

"Go ahead then, call the police. What are you going to tell them? That you and your in-laws were killed by vampires. That you are now in the protection of an ancient dragon lady and her militia? They will pass you off as a prank call," she said.

"I'll tell them you have kidnapped me and my children," he said.

"Do you know what will happen then? Your information will be passed on to organisations that aim to find you. These organisations have been infiltrated by vampires. Those vampires will then use the information to hunt you and your children down. They have one motive. To kill you, all three of you. I'm not making this up John. Pick up a phone and see what happens," she said.

John's head spun as he tried to absorb all the information. His life had changed dramatically over the past four months. And now in the last hour the world he thought he understood had changed beyond recognition. He felt like he was going to be sick and he stumbled under the weight of the situation. Andra caught him and steadied him.

"You have to help me, please. Michael and Sue were all the family we had left. My Mum and Dad died years ago. Please! You have to help us!" he said.

"That is exactly why we have brought you here. This is your home now. I know it's not a house but it is safe and you have all you could ever need here. You are my guests and everyone here will protect you. Now let's get you all down to the medical bay. You all need a check-up and your wounds need treating," she said.

John smiled and a tear of hope ran down his face.

Chapter 8.

John and the twins spent the next few days together in the medical bay. Andra visited them three or four times a day. As she had already expected John had a lot of questions and she answered them all to the best of her ability.

"Do you know everything about vampires?" he said when she visited on the second afternoon.

"Well, I have studied them for many years. I know a lot but there are still some things that I don't know. What's on your mind?" she said.

"I'm still trying to understand this, but from what you told me and what I have seen with my own eyes, it's clear that Vincent is different. I'm still coming to terms with the idea of vampires being real too. So, admitting that my son is one is difficult, but it would explain some things. Is that why he is growing so fast?" he said.

"Yes, from what I have seen vampires grow at more or less five times the rate of humans. So in one year he will be the size five year old. He will hit puberty at about two to three years and will be fully grown at five years old. By then he will look about twenty-five. At that point, or thereabouts, he will stop aging," she said.

"Bloody hell, that's a lot of growth in a short space of time," he said.

"Yeah, for a human, but he's not human. He just looks a lot like one. Some people think that vampires are the next stage of human evolution, Homo Superior if you like, but they're not. They're a different species in many ways," she said.

"He's still my son though. I don't care what he is, I still love him and will take care of him as long as he needs me to," he said.

Andra smiled and placed her hand on John's.

"Yes, he will always be your son," she said.

"The stopping aging at twenty-five is a pretty sweet deal," he said with a smile.

"Yes, it's also a good way to tell the bitten vampires from the born vampires. The bitten ones stay the age they were when they were made. The born ones will be around their mid-twenties and are more dangerous than the bitten variety," she said.

Chapter 9.

As the months passed John began to get used to living in the warehouse. He enjoyed spending time with Andra and working with the soldiers. He put his knowledge as a mechanic to good use by helping to fix the vehicles in the garage and doing basic maintenance jobs.

One morning he and the mechanics were talking and laughing while exchanging anecdotes. Andra came in to see how they were doing.

"Can I ask a question, Andra?" said John.

"Of course. What is on your mind?" she said.

"Who are the S.O.V.E.U.? Erm… I mean where do you find the soldiers and how do they join?" he said.

"They are mercenaries. Some are regular army, some are ex S.A.S. and S.B.S. Others are ex-Delta force, Navy Seals and Black Ops. They have all seen active service and have fought against vampires at some point in their lives. To apply they have to either already be retired from active service or put in an application to their superior officers. If their application is approved they then come to one of my private training facilities where they go through a rigorous three-day assessment," she said.

"What type of assessment?" he said.

"They have to pass a medical evaluation, a physical fitness test, a mental proficiency test, a weapons proficiency test, and finally an interview," she said.

"So it's tough then?" he said.

"Damn right it's tough. Sorts the soldiers from the civvies," said one of the mechanics with a big smile on his face.

"Yes it's tough, it needs to be, we're fighting vampires. There is no other enemy like them. They are faster, stronger, and smarter than any other enemy a soldier will face," said Andra.

"How do you afford to hire all these ex-soldiers?" said John.

"I've had a lot of time to save a lot of money," she said.

"So it's a private army?" he said.

"Not necessarily, I own and run the S.O.V.E.U. and have done for many years. We have connections with the military and The Ministry of Defence. Though, if you tried to find those connections all knowledge would be denied and they would even deny our existence," she said.

"Is it…erm…is it possible that someone who isn't ex-military could be trained to be part of the…erm," he said.

Andra looked at him and raised her eyebrows, "Part of the S.O.V.E.U.?" she said.

"Yes," said John.

"Are you saying you want to train with us, join my team and possibly fight alongside my unit?" she said as she folded her arms infront of her.

"Yes, ma'am. Well, maybe not be a soldier, but I do need to be able to protect my kids," he said.

"You think you could handle it?" she said.

"Yes Ma'am, I do," he said.

She turned to the rest of the mechanics.

"What do you guys think?" she said.

"I think you should let him train with us. Give him a chance to prove himself. He seems confident enough," said one of them.

"Yes. Let him put his money where his mouth is. You know, test his mettle," said another with a smile.

"Hmm," Andra eyed him up and down. She pouted her lips slightly as she mulled over the request.

"Ok, John. I'll train you. I'm not going to go easy on you though. It's going to be hard and it's going to test your limits but remember, you did ask for this. Tomorrow morning in the training gym at nine," she said.

"Yes, ma'am," said John with a wide smile.

The next morning John got up at 8 am and got the kids washed and dressed. He fed Alex a bottle of milk but Vincent still refused to drink or eat anything. He would cry and fight whenever he was offered food or drink. Despite this, he was still growing and gaining weight. He now looked more like a human at 10 months old rather than the 2 months old that he was.

John then left them with Tess, who had previously trained in child care before she joined the army. It was the first time he had been away from his children and he felt anxious about leaving them with her. He knew he could trust these people so he tried to relax. He went down to the training gym at 9 am.

Andra was already there. He watched her for a moment as she ran up the wall then backflipped from it and landed in almost the centre of the large square room.

"I hope you don't expect me to do that," he said with a smile.

"No, you learn that tomorrow," she said and smiled back at him.

Suddenly his smile wasn't quite so big.

"I'm joking," she said.

"Yes, um, yea I knew that. So what are we doing today?" he said.

"Well, that depends. Have you ever done any form of sports or fitness training?" she said.

"I used to play cricket and I go to the gym twice a week," he said.

"Good. We can work with that. So first of all we need to get your fitness up, then we will start for real," she said.

"How long will that take?" he said.

"We train every day for eight weeks," she said.

"Ok," he said.

"For five hours a day," she said and smiled.

"Um…ok, ok I can do that," he said with a slightly worried look.

"Hey, you want to be in my unit. This is what you have to do," she said.

"Yes that is what I want," he said.

"Ok, let's get started then," she said and slapped him on the shoulder.

The weeks passed by slowly at first but after a while John +started to enjoy himself. He could feel his body getting stronger and healthier. On the last day of the eighth week he walked into the training room and Andra was stood in the centre with a smile on her face.

"Why are you so happy," he said.

"Because today we add something new to your training," she said.

"Dare I ask what this something might be?" he said.

"Martial arts, starting with Karate," she said then clapped her hands and rubbed them together. "Ok let us begin."

In the eight months that followed she taught him as much as she could; including elements of Jiu-Jitsu, Taijutsu, Aikido, Kendo, Thai boxing, Jeet Kune Do, Judo, and Ninjitsu.

"Where did you learn all these techniques?" he asked.

"After I was attacked by Ruhsarr I began to change. My smooth skin became scales and my fingernails became claws. I was chased out of my hometown and every town I came across after that. Soon it wasn't just towns but countries. Eventually, I found myself in what is now China during the Xia dynasty. That was a little over four thousand years ago and by that time I looked like I do now. They respected their dragons in those days, they still do, though not a lot of people believe dragons are real anymore," she said.

"So they taught you to defend yourself?" said John.

"Yes, I also defended the people in the towns I ruled. They looked to me as a representative of their Gods on Earth. Back then China was divided into hundreds of small citadels and towns that were constantly at war. If a town was invaded the leader of that town would be killed. I had to know how to fight, just being strong and fast isn't enough. You need techniques and disciplines. You need to be able to focus your attacks while at the same time being capable of defending yourself from attacks. So they taught me every technique they knew. I soaked up the knowledge they imparted unto me like a sponge. I then learned how to use and smith blades and how to build architecture with the materials that were available in that age. In the years since I have made a point to learn every new discipline I have come across. I have taught you elements of disciplines that you will be able to utilise to their greatest effect," she said.

"Thank you, Ma'am. I greatly appreciate you teaching me," he said.

"Talking about teaching, tomorrow I want to train you in the use of combat weaponry," she said.

"Yes Ma'am," he said.
He smiled at the thought of this. He had never expected to ever learn anything like this and felt like he was in a movie.

"Good, see you tomorrow morning," she said.

The next day when he arrived at the training room Andra had set up two weapons racks with Bo staffs, Naginata, Odachi, and Katana.

"Wow. Are we going to use those today? I mean, I don't think I'm ready to use swords yet," said John.

"Don't worry, they are training weapons. The blades are blunt but they are made of the same metals as the real thing so you get a feel for the weight of the weapons right from the start,"

"Oh. That's good to know. I plan on keeping all my extremities as long as I can," he said.

"Yeah, I don't want you to go losing your head in the literal sense," she said with a laugh.

As the months passed Andra taught him more hand to hand combat. She also taught him not only how to wield a sword but the many fighting techniques that had been devised around them. She soon added how to shoot with all types of guns and rifles. She taught him how to clean and maintain the weapons too. On top of that, he learned about ballistics, explosives, and incendiary weapons. Throughout his training she taught him the history of vampires and their lore.

Chapter 10.

Another eight months had passed and John was training with Andra in one of the gyms. They were stood in the centre of one of the huge blue padded mats. The racks of training weapons that they had used up to now were nowhere to be seen. Along one of the walls on the mounted weapon racks were swords, staffs, axes and other handheld weapons.

Andra's eyes were stern and serious as she looked right into John. He would have been a liar if he had said that she didn't scare him with this expression.

"Ok, it is time. We're going to see how you fare in real fight situations. Like we discussed," said Andra.

"What sort of fight situations?" said John as a wave of anxiety swept over him.

"We'll start with a one on one, ground based situation as that is the most realistic situation you'll find yourself in. Now, most humans don't know that vampires exist and won't expect an assailant to be anywhere near as strong," she said.

"They'll just think that attacker is human until it's too late," he said.

"Exactly," said Andra pointing a friendly finger at him. "In the same way the vampires won't be expecting a powerful attack from a human," she said.

"So, how are we starting?" he said.
Andra ran at him fast, shoulder barged him, and knocked him off his feet. He hit the floor and lay still while she stood and looked at him.

"Vampires will use their abilities to move quick and silent. They won't hesitate about using them against you.

The element of surprise has worked for thousands of years and it always will," she said.

John lay on the floor and wheezed for a moment, When he'd caught his breath he got to his feet.

"What the hell was that for?" he said.

Andra punched him square in the face.

"Seriously, Andra! What the fuck?!" he said with a bloodied nose.

"Stop complaining and defend yourself," she said.

She punched him again, harder this time.

"Stop punching me!" he said in a broken voice.

Andra grabbed him by the throat and roared in his face.

"Defend yourself!"

She spun him around and threw him across the room. He hit the floor and the momentum slid him to the wall. She walked at him, her eyes were focused and all the muscles in her shoulders tensed as her hands clenched in fists. John got to his feet, grabbed a stick from the wall and swung it at her legs. She jumped over it, he swung it back again, and again she jumped over it. He swung the stick at her body this time, but she caught the end and pulled it out of his hands then threw it aside. He ran alongside the wall and snatched a Naginata from the rack. He turned back towards Andra and swung the end without the blade towards her head. It hit its mark and she stumbled slightly to the left but kept on walking towards him.

"Harder," she said. "Each hit has got to be hard enough to debilitate or kill."

"I don't want to hurt you," said John.

"Hit me!" she roared.

He jabbed the blunt end of the pole hard into her face

but still she kept coming. He hit her across the ribs, in the stomach, across the abdomen, across the thighs and then he jabbed the weapon forward directly into her chin and put all his weight behind it. Her head flew back and when her face came down her eyes were staring right at him. She snarled and roared at him. He swung the Naginata again she caught it and tore it out of his hands then threw it in his direction. The blade sliced the air as it passed his ear and buried itself in the wall ten feet behind him.

"What the fuck?!" said John.

His voice was fraught with anger and shock as his eyes followed the weapon.

He looked back just as Andra grabbed him by the throat. She lifted him from the floor and slammed him into the wall. She roared again, her mouth was inches from his face and gaping wide. Her hot breath rasped against his skin, her teeth were huge and a little flicker of flame burst from her nostrils.

"If I was a vampire you would already be dead. If you had hit a vampire as hard as you hit me they would be dazed and confused but not dead. Every blow has to be hard, precise and most of all, deadly. Hard is not good enough, it needs to be the hardest you can muster. You need to be shattering bones, cracking skulls, and killing with every single blow. I have told you what your children mean to the world. There may come a time when you are their sole protector! If you die, they die! Get it?!" she said.

"I didn't want to hurt you though," he said.

He felt the hand she had around his neck loosened and she put him down.

"Oh John, you won't hurt me. I've fought the best warriors that Genghis Khan, the Romans, ancient Greeks, Persians, and more could throw at me. I've battled armies, both human and vampire. I've been burned, boiled, stabbed, shot, crushed, and blown up more times than I care to remember. I've survived every method of killing that you can think of. You can't hurt me but I want you to fight like you can," she said. She placed her hands on his shoulders and smiled. She then turned, walked back to the centre of the room, and turned to face him again.

"Now let's try again and this time use the weapons to their full potential," she said.

John looked at her. He found her attractive when she smiled, but she still scared the shit out of him.

"I'm glad you're on my side," he said.

And she laughed.

Chapter 11.

Three months later Alex was still growing at a normal child's rate. He was one and a half years old. Vincent was now the size of a seven year old, and was hitting targets far above his age range. He would eat raw meat as it was the only thing other than blood that he could digest. Andra had her scientists run both tissue and physical health test on him.

One afternoon John was doing his laundry in the communal laundry area when she came into his to talk to him about the results.

"What did they say about him?" said John.

"They ran an array of tests on him. The first thing they noted is that he is a first-generation vampire," said Andra.

"What does that mean?" said John.

"Well, it means that he can survive in direct sunlight sun for a short time. Too long though and he will succumb to the effect like any other vampire. Don't ever let him bite anyone. One bite from him will turn them into a vampire without the need for them to drink any of his blood," she said.

"Wow, that's pretty serious. Is there anything else?" he said.

"Yes, they let him have a go at a full size assault course. He's fast, agile, and incredibly strong. He completed the course in seventeen minutes on the dot. The fastest any full grown human adult has been around there is nineteen minutes forty. I have my own personal running machine, it has been specifically made for me. They clocked him at just under seventy miles per hour.

He can jump over twenty feet straight up from standing and can lift just under a ton," she said.

"Fuckin' hell, how is that possible?" he said.

"Vampires are incredibly dangerous, even from an early age," she said with a shrug.

"That's crazy," he said.

"Damn right it is. I've been hunting vampires a long time but he could leave some of them in the dust and he's still a child. That last of it either, academically he is way above human standards. I'd go as far as to say he's of child genius levels," she said.

"What do we do now?" he said.

"We're going to have to design an educational program for him. I think a physical program will be useful too. He has a lot of energy that needs to be focused in the right direction. I'll start working on it as soon as I can.

Two days later John, Vincent, and Alex were sat at the kitchen table in the quarters that Andra had given them to live in. The living area was set out like a normal three bedroom flat. As well as the bedrooms it had, a living room with a T.V., stereo, a fully equipped kitchen, and bathroom complete with a full sized bath. There was also an on-suite bathroom off from John's bedroom with a shower cubical. The walls were solid concrete painted white but because of the lack of windows it didn't disguise the fact they were underground.

They were sat at the kitchen table and watching something on TV while they ate their evening meal. John was planning to put Alex to bed when they were finished. The child who was one year and nine months old sat in his highchair. He happily ate two chicken nuggets cut into quarters and chopped vegetables. John had a roast chicken pie and chips. He had given Vincent, who was now the size of an eight year old human, a raw steak and a glass of pigs' blood. John hated feeding him like this but he loved his son. This was the only thing Vincent could eat, and John couldn't stand to see him starve. He'd tried to feed the boy cooked meats and vegetables but it made him projectile vomit and horribly ill for two days.

"Daddy?" said Vincent looking up from his plate.

"Yes son?" said John.

"I was reading a book this morning, it had a mummy, a daddy, and a son in it," said Vincent.

"Yes," said John, he knew the boy was about to ask a difficult question.

"You have told me about my mummy before. What happened to her?" said Vincent

"She died just after you were born, son," said John.

"I know, I mean how did she die?" said Vincent
John looked down and closed his eyes. He had expected these questions but he didn't ever think he would be discussing them with his son at such a young age. The pains of grief had only faded a little since Annabelle's death but he had to continue despite all he was feeling. He lifted his head, opened his eyes and fought back the tears.

"She was attacked by a bad man a few days before you were born. Having a baby is difficult and when she gave birth to you and your brother she was very poorly and weak and she died," said John.
As he spoke his voice wobbled as he tried to keep his

composure.

He didn't try to soften the truth with Vincent. The boy was so astute he had seen through any sugar coating on any explanation or lies John had told him. He would just keep on asking until he got to the truth.

"Is that why I'm the way I am? Because mummy was attacked?" said Vincent.

"What do you mean the way you are?" said John.

"You know, different," said Vincent.

"No son, you're not different, you're special," said John.

"Dad, I know I'm different. Alex and me are the same age, yet I'm walking and talking while he has only recently learnt to walk and most of his speech is still baby babble," said Vincent.

"The man who attacked your mum was extremely strong. Andra says he was not a normal person. You are…unique like her. She says you and Alex are very special," said John.

Vincent looked as if he was going to ask another question but then his face softened.

"I wish mummy was still alive," he said.

John couldn't fight his emotions anymore and the tears rolled down his face,

"So do I son. So do I," he said.

Vincent jumped down from his chair and walked around the table to his dad. He then climbed up onto his knee and hugged him.

"I'm sorry, I didn't mean to make you cry, daddy," he said.

"It ok, son, I probably don't cry enough," said John.

Chapter 12.

Monday 15th June 1998

A year and a half passed and things got easier for John. He got counselling and seeing the kids grow helped him deal with his grief. Having more responsibilities also helped to keep his mind focused on other things.

He, Vincent, and Alex lived almost exclusively in the warehouse complex. Anything they needed was bought in for them. As the boys were growing up they needed toys, games, and educational material.

Alex was an average three year old who liked to play with toys, watch kid's television shows, ask questions and make a mess.

Vincent looked like a 15 year old. He would read everything he could get his hands on, watched all sorts of films in any language, and he liked to listen to all types of music; but mostly he liked heavy metal.

It was three in the morning and they were all in their beds when there was a knock at the door of their quarters. The second knock was heavier and the door handle rattled. For a moment everything was silent, then the door burst open, bending the lock and splintering the frame. Andra rushed in, ran into John's room, grabbed him, and shook him awake.

"John! John, get up! We've got to move! They've found us!" she said.

"What? Who?" said John as he groggily opened his eyes.

"A group of stalkers have found the warehouse. We

have to get you out of here!" she said.

"Ok, ok, erm, ok," said John as he jumped out of bed, pulled on his jeans and began throwing clothes into a bag. "Er, what the hell are stalkers?" he said as he realised what Andra had said.

"Stalkers are bad mother fuckers. They're a vampire special unit. Basically, they're assassins. They hunt down any target they have been hired to kill. Most probably hired by Ruhsarr as he has deduced by now that we found you. There have been attacks on two other local bases in the past few months. I'm assuming that after the failed attack on your home they are using that location as a central point and working their way out. Whatever the situation, we can't let them find you here," she spoke fast as she stuffed some of the children's clothes into a holdall.

John ran into Alex's room, woke him up, and lifted him out of his bed. He began to cry and reached for his favourite teddy. John picked up the toy and put it in Alex's hands. The boy hugged it tight to his chest and his cries turn to mumbles of annoyance as he buried his face in John's chest. Meanwhile Andra ran to Vincent's room where she found him awake and listening to albums through a pair of headphones. She grabbed him by the shoulder. He turned around startled and pulled off the headphones.

"Come on Vince. We've got to go," she said.

"It's three in the morning, where are we going at this time!?" he said in a whine.

"I haven't got time for your attitude Vincent! Grab some clothes, your cd player, put them in a bag, and get your arse in the living room," she said.

He got to his feet, grabbed a holdall and filled it with his possessions, then ran into the living room. He knew Andra was not the type who would ask twice.

"Where are we going?" he whined to John.

"Just do as Andra says, Vincent!" he said.

"Now follow me," she said and led them out of the door.

As they moved up the corridor a soldier quickly strode towards them. He had short cropped hair, pointy features, and was of a medium build.

"You asked for me specifically, Ma'am?" he said as he addressed Andra.

"Yes Raynor, come with us. I have an extremely important mission for you," she said.

"Ok Ma'am," he said.

"John this is Raynor, Raynor this is John." They both nodded and smiled. "John, Raynor is going to take you all out of here in a car. I hope you have everything that you need because you will not be coming back here," she said.

"We're not coming back here?" said John.

"No, I am having you evacuated. You're not safe here anymore," she said.

"Ok Ma'am," he said.

He was a little puzzled by this but knew Andra well enough by now to know she didn't just take actions on a whim.

"Raynor, I want you to take John, Vincent, and Alex to RAF Woodvale in Liverpool. I'm putting Project Nomad into operation and I selected you because you are the best driver we have. You understand the severity of this mission. You go fast, but don't draw attention to yourselves, and most of all don't stop for anything. Do not come back here for any reason. Go straight to the airbase. There will be a private plane ready and prepped for take-off. John, you and the boys get on that plane. A friend of mine, Major Owens, will be there to accompany you. There will be details of your destination and instructions of what to do when you arrive there," said Andra.

"Yes Ma'am," said John.

They had walked up a flight of stairs and along a corridor. A group of soldiers ran passed them and they could hear gunfire from the floors above. Andra opened a door and they followed her into the garage level. She stepped into a small office, opened a cabinet, and took out a set of keys.

"Take the Audi S4," she said to Raynor as she threw them to him.

He caught them, unlocked the car, opened the door, and climbed in. He adjusted the seat, then the rear-view mirror, and started the ignition. He ran his hands around the outside edge wheel to get a feel for the car in an almost subconscious ritual. There was already a baby seat in the back of the car. John put Alex in it and fasten his seatbelt. Vincent got in the other side while Andra opened the boot and threw in the bags. John then started to get in the back, Andra placed her hand on his shoulder and he turned to look at her.

"What are you doing John?" she said.

"I'm getting in the car," he said.

"I mean, why are you getting in the back?" she said.

"So that you can get in the front. You need more room," he said.

"I'm not coming with you, John. I can't, I've got to lead all my soldiers and deal with these stalkers. If they found any evidence you were here then got away and told anyone there would be no telling how many vampires there would be hunting you," she said.

"But we need you," he said as tears welled in his eyes.

"You're ready, John, you can protect them. Just keep your head down and don't draw attention. If you have to fight remember your training and make every hit count," she said then pulled him close and hugged him tightly. "Now go."

"Thank you for everything you have done for us," said John and kissed her on the cheek.

He then shut the rear door and got into the front passenger seat and put on his seatbelt. Andra closed to door for him and forced a smile onto her face as she held back her own tears.

"Seatbelt, Vincent," said John.

"I'd advise it," said Raynor.

Vincent sighed as he rolled his eyes but was soon scrambling to fasten his belt as the car shot away from the parking space. They sped out through a secret garage door and onto the streets of Salford.

"I will see you again, John," said Andra.

As she sent them out from under her protective wing she didn't know what they would face. She did know it was better than they stayed here and running the risk of being captured.

She then turned, ran back to the stairs and up to the warehouse level. She swung her Colt C7A2 automatic rifle from her shoulder and switched off the safety. As she ran along the corridor a stalker had one of her soldiers by the neck and was about to bite him. With an inhuman precision she shot ten rounds into its head and heart. The soldier fell to the floor and the stalker's ash-filled clothes fell on top of him. He quickly batted them away and jumped to his feet.

"You ok, Barlow?" she said.

"Yes, Ma'am. Thank you, Ma'am," he said.

"Don't mention it. Carry on soldier," she said.

She continued on her way and ran onto the ground floor of the warehouse. The humans and vampires had stacked up crates and steel barrels. They now took cover behind these in different parts of the expansive room. As she moved through the building a stalker lunged at her. Without missing a beat she raised her leg up infront of her and jumped straight at it. Her foot struck the vampire's throat and she stomped it down to the ground. Blood gurgled in the vampire's mouth. She stamped her other foot down, crushing the vampire's skull and splattering its brains over the floor. The body burned up as she moved on.

She approached a group of soldiers who were hunkered down behind a makeshift barrier of crates and barrels.

"What you got, Jones?" she said in a whisper to one of the soldiers.

"One of the fuckers has barricaded itself in back there behind that wall and the steel drums. The wall is six inches thick. We're not gonna get to it whilst it's dug in like that. It shot Lackey. He's alive but injured. It's using him as bait," he said and gestured towards a soldier who lay crying out in pain about twenty feet away between the soldiers and the vampire. "Anyone who has tried to help him has been fired upon. It's already killed Lex and Smithy too," he said.

"Guerrilla tactics huh," she said.

"Yes, Ma'am. Clever little fucker this one," said Jones.

"How long has he been there?" she said.

"Lackey or the blood sucking ballbag?" said the Jones.

"Both," she said.

"Roughly fifteen minutes, Ma'am," said Jones.

"Must be desperate to be pulling this shit," she said and took a moment to think. "Ok, listen, we're going to take control of the situation. I'll jump out of cover, run over to Lackey and slide him back towards you. He'll need a medic ASAP. When the vampire steps out of cover to shoot me you all hit it with everything you have," she said.

"Yes Ma'am," said all the soldiers.

"Ready?" She said.

They all nodded then pointed their guns in the direction of the vampire. They let out a few short bursts. The stalker hunkered down and took cover. Andra used that moment to vault out from her position behind the crates and run towards Lackey. The stalker leaned out and shot at Andra, the bullets hit their mark but she kept on moving. The soldiers shot at the vampire but it ducked back down again. Andra made it to Lackey and was about to slide him away to safety when a bullet punctured his skull. She looked at the now dead body of Lackey in her hands then up at the stalker. The blood raced through her veins and her face twisted up with a deep set anger. She stood up took a deep breath and roared as loud as she could. The Stalker shot at her in vain, knowing bullets were useless. She set off charging directly at it as the bones of her face and jaw extended and clicked into a new position. The stalker's heart beat like it was going to come out of its chest. It managed to control its nerves enough to throw down the rifle and swing the RPG launcher down from its shoulder. Andra took a deep breath and spat a huge fireball right at it. The flames engulfed the vampire and everything around it. She grabbed its writhing, burning body and breathed more fire right into what was left of its face. That's when RPG in the launcher exploded. Chunks of Andra and burning stalker flew in all directions.

Chapter 13.

They only saw three other cars on the roads as the Audi S4 sped through the streets of Manchester. Raynor drove so fast that the street lights shone through the windows like strobe lights. They turned onto the motorway and headed in the direction of Formby. After about forty minutes they reached their destination and turned left into the entrance of airbase RAF Woodvale. Raynor eased his foot onto the brake pedal and slowed the car as they approached the white and red gates. A guard with a sullen face stepped out from the green gatehouse and into the road. He held up his hand and Raynor complied and stopped the car feet from him. The guard walked up to the car as the window wound down with an electronic hum. Raynor opened his wallet, took out his I.D. card and passed it to the guard for inspection.

"What's your business here, Sergeant Raynor?" said the guard as he inspected the card.

"I'm delivering the package for Project Nomad, Private Simmons," said Raynor as he noted the soldier's name tag.

Simmons looked at the card again, then at Raynor, John and the two boys in the back. He passed the I.D. card back to Raynor, then reached up and clicked the button on his chest-mounted radio.

"Major Owens. The package you expected has arrived," he said.

"Good, let them in," crackled a voice over the radio. Simmons stepped into the gatehouse, raised the gate, and waved them through.

"The plane is ready on the runway, Major Owens is already aboard. Straight up this road, then right. You'll see the plane on the runway," he said.

John smiled at the soldier who didn't return the gesture. Not even the corners of his mouth curled up.

"Thank you Private," said Raynor and wound the window up.

"He's a happy chap isn't he," said John with a smile as they drove on.

"Gate duty does that to you," said Raynor with a laugh.

He drove into the airfield then turned right to the runway. They saw the light from the windows of the private plane. As they got closer they could see a tall well-built man stood just outside the boarding door. The car's headlights illuminated him and they could see that he wore a Major's uniform. Raynor slowed the car and stopped next to the plane. He stepped out of the car, followed by Vincent and John who retrieved Alex from the rear seat. Two soldiers got the bags from the back of the car and began loading them into the baggage hold of the plane. Raynor walked over to the Major and saluted him. Major Owens saluted him back then held his hand out and Raynor shook it.

"Hello, Sergeant Raynor. Your arrival is expected but we weren't expecting you quite so soon," he said with a broad smile.

"Hello, Sir. I think the events of this morning are a surprise to us all," said Raynor as he tried to put the same enthusiasm into his smile.

The Major turned his attention to John.

"Ah, John Austin. I'm Major Owens. Andra has told

me a lot about you and your family. Yours is an unusual situation, yes, very unusual indeed. The military has a close but confidential connection with Andra and has done for many years. There is a steady alliance between our two organisations. I have known her for almost twenty years myself. She has kept the existence of your family a closely guarded secret. She only told me two months ago," he said.

"Yes, she has told me it's all very hush hush. Though I suppose a situation like ours would have to be," said John.

"Indeed, we deal with the things that need to be kept out of the public domain," said Owens. He then looked at Raynor. "Sergeant Raynor, thank you for your services, you can return to your station now."

"Yes, sir, thank you, sir," said Raynor.
He then got back in the car and drove away to the airfield control station.

"Ok John, we've got no time to waste. There are people waiting for us," said Owens then climbed aboard. John picked up Alex, and Vincent followed them as they boarded the plane. Owens then closed the door and they made their way through the plane.

"Take a seat and put your seatbelt on, son. There will be a film on the TV soon. There are headphones in the back of the seat infront of you," said Owens to Vincent.

"Uh-huh," mumbled Vincent as he fished his personal CD player from his coat pocket and slumped into one of the seats.

"Vince, put your seatbelt on," said John in a stern tone. He fastened Alex's seatbelt while the small boy squirmed and whined.

"Right," said Vincent with a sigh.

"Lose the attitude, Vincent!" barked John.

Vincent didn't respond, he just bunged in his earphones and hit play on the CD player. The music of Ozzy Osbourne burst to life in his head.

Alex now settled in the seat and Owens invited John to sit down at a table a few seats back. The pilot asked the air traffic controller for permission to take off and it was granted. The plane taxied into position on the runway. It then accelerated, the front landing gear lifted off the tarmac closely followed by the rear and the plane took off into the early morning sky.

When they reached twenty thousand feet Owens took a slim, brushed steel briefcase from under his seat and placed it on the table between them. He opened it, took out a file marked 'Top Secret' and placed that on the table. He closed the briefcase and placed it back beneath his seat. He slid the file across the table so that it sat directly infront of John.

"What's this?" he asked as he looked at the file.

"Inside you will find all the details of Project Nomad and everything you will need to know. Read it carefully, it will answer all your questions. I don't know everything in there as Project Nomad has been entirely devised by Andra," said Owens.

John opened the file and inside he found a neatly printed dossier. The first page read 'EXTREMELY TOP SECRET!' The next two pages were written in Andra's precise cursive handwriting and addressed directly to John. It read:

"My dearest John.

You are probably wondering why you have no previous knowledge of Project Nomad. The simple reason for this is that I couldn't let you know anything because it had to be kept secret. I couldn't let anyone know but a handful of people.

If you are reading this the location of base 115 has been compromised. I don't know if the agency who have attained this knowledge realise that the warehouse has also been acting as your safe house. Just know that I had to get you, Alex, and Vincent, out of the reach of any vampires. I have arranged this flight for just such a purpose. There is no flight number on this plane as it is classed as a secret military flight. The plane is set to land at a private military airbase in Toulouse, France.

You can trust Major Owens, he is an old friend of mine and has fought vampires by my side on many occasions. He has also seen active service in many secret missions, so there isn't much that can shock him. He will be traveling with you on this mission.
The flight is only 1 hour 45 minutes. When you land I have arranged for there to be a motorhome or recreational vehicle, as they are sometimes known, waiting for you. It will look mundane but that is entirely intentional. You don't want you to stand out as anything but tourists. In fact we want you to blend in seamlessly. Inside it is custom built for all your needs. I have drawn a diagnostic of the layout of the vehicle and have included it in this dossier. Certain areas within it contain concealed weapons compartments all of which are shown and labelled in the diagnostic. Do not worry though, if the vehicle has to be searched by customs or

any other authority for any reason the compartments are completely hidden.

I have opened a bank account for you. There will be the equivalent of £200 deposited into it on a daily basis. This account, the money within it, the account from where the money has been deposited and the location you withdraw the money from are all completely untraceable so you can use it without worry.

I have had new passports made for all four of you. Owens and you also have new driver's licences. Although the identities are false the passports and cards are all genuine and can be checked by the authorities without suspicion. They cannot be traced back to the military, the S.O.V.E.U., or your true identities. However, the right people in the right places will know who you are if you need assistance. These bank cards, driver's licences, and passports are all enclosed within the envelope in the back of this file.

Your cover story is you are a family. You and Vincent are brothers due to him now looking too old to be your son. Alex is your son and Owens is your uncle. If anyone asks, you are on holiday and just passing through.

When I first met you I told you Alex is the key to all this. It is up to you to protect him, he is the one the vampire prophecy talks of. According to their lore, he is the bringer of their apocalypse. As of yet, I am not sure how that might be or what abilities he may possess. However, I do know that they are scared of what he will be able to do so they want him dead. For this reason, if not any other, he must live. You must protect him above all others, even yourself. If that be with your last breathe then so be it. Vincent is a strong, intelligent, and capable man who can fend for himself. Despite this I know you will protect him too.

Travel by daylight when the vampires are less of a threat and rest in the dark hours. To do this you will have to set up a rota between you and Owens to take watch when you set up camp for the night. Vincent will soon be old enough to take watch too. You must be alert and able, so take it in turns to rest and drive in the daytime when you can.

Never use your real names when in the company of other people as you never know who might be listening. Never stay in one place more than one day as you never know who might be watching.

This is going to be hard for you to read but I have to warn you nevertheless. Vampires prefer the company of their own kind and Vincent may want to leave when he reaches full maturity. No matter how positive your relationship is with him there may be nothing you can do to stop this.

Finally, Project Nomad is only a temporary solution, I will send word when the threat is over.

All my love, your friend
Andra x"

The next page was an extremely precise hand-drawn layout of the vehicle as Andra had described in her letter. To John, it looked like a large camper van. 'Yep that is mundane.' he thought to himself.

The diagram was labelled in Andra's handwriting. The weapons compartments were located throughout the vehicle. Long guns and automatic rifles were under the floors in the bedrooms. There are 2 Remington combat shotguns, 2 Colt C7A2s, and 2 MP5s.

The handguns were racked in compartments in the wall of the vehicle behind the driver and passenger seats. Four modified MP-443s, two Smith and Weston .44 magnums, and four micro-Uzis.
All the guns had their corresponding, silver-coated ammunition.

In the floor in the middle of the lounge area in the vehicle was a compartment with swords and bladed weapons. It contained Four Katanas, two Odachi, two Naginata, and sharpening stones.

The outer shell of the vehicle was labelled as Kevlar coated titanium with a rigid titanium chassis. The wheels were titanium and the tyres were rubber with an inner Kevlar weave making them bulletproof.

"This thing is built to be tough," he said to Owens as he passed him the diagnostic.

"Bloody hell. It's essentially an armoured vehicle," Owens replied as he looked it over.

John found the envelope, that Andra had mentioned in the letter, tucked safely at the back of the folder. He opened it, took out the documents and the passports and opened one. Inside there was a picture of Vincent. The name beside it was Vincent Brooks with 14/5/1981 as the date of birth.

"The date on Vincent's passport would make him seventeen. I'm twenty-seven so that would mean there are only ten years between us," said John.

He opened another and passed it to Owens,

"Hello Uncle Anthony," said John with a laugh.

He looked at the two other passports his read 'John Brooks' and Alex was now 'Alex Brooks'. He took out the cash card and the pin number that were together in a resealable bag and placed them on the table. He took out the driving licence documents, passed Owens his and folded his own and put it +inside his wallet. He tapped Vincent on the shoulder,

"Yes," said Vincent with a tone.

"I'm getting tired of telling you not to take that tone with me," said John.

"Sorry dad," he said sheepishly.

"This is your new passport," said John as he passed it to him.

"I already have a passport," said Vincent.

"I know you do but this is a new one. We all have new ones, we've been given new names to protect our identities. We're going to France, we'll be incognito," John said with a smile.

"Cool," said Vincent.

"You might want to learn to speak some French," said John.

"Yep, already do," said Vincent.

"You do? How much?" said John.

"Erm, most of it I think," said Vincent.

"Most of the language?" said John as he raised his eyebrows in surprise.

"Yes, I think so. Not including colloquialisms and slang, obviously, but enough to hold a competent conversation," said Vincent

"When did you do that?" said John.

"I've read books, listened to music, and watched films," said Vincent with a shrug.

"And you know most of the language?" said John as he tried not to sound too condescending.

"I don't sleep like you do, Dad. I have a lot more time on my hands," said Vincent.

"Oh yes, sorry son. That's good, that's good," he said and placed his hand on Vincent's shoulder.

He then sat down in the seat next to Alex who was now happily playing with a toy car and a plastic triceratops.

"Are you having fun?" he said as he ruffled the boy's hair.

"Yeeeaahh!" said Alex excitedly.

"Who's this?" said John pointing to the dinosaur.

"He a ceritopsss. He attakin the car," said Alex.

"Is he the bad guy then?" said John.

"No, he goodie, car is baaad," said Alex as he shook his head.

"OK, naughty car," said John which made Alex giggle. A splinter of sadness pierced John's heart. 'If only Annabelle was here to see them.' he thought.

"The film is starting," said Owens.

"Ugh boring," Vincent said without even waiting to see the title of the film. He turned up his CD player and slid down into his chair.

Chapter 14.

John was woken by the pilot's voice through the intercom.

"We are making our final approach and will be landing in approximately five minutes, gentlemen. Please put on your seatbelts."

The plane made a shallow bank to the left and began to descend. Alex began to cry and the pressure built up in his ears so John unwrapped a sweet and offered it to him. Alex shook his head as tears welled in his eyes.

"It will make the pain go away," said John.
Alex opened his mouth so John could pop in the sweet. As he swallowed his ears popped and the pain went away.

"Better now?" said John.
Alex nodded his head and smiled. The pilot applied the airbrakes and the plane began to level out as it came in to land. The tyres squealed as they hit the tarmac of the runway. The plane slowed then came to a gradual halt.

"Thanks for flying with secret airways. It is 0630 hours French time. This isn't a commercial flight. Please remember to take all your belongings with you and collect your luggage from the hold. Anything left behind will be mine by default. Now get off my plane," said the pilot in a jovial tone.
John and Owens laughed.

As they exited the plane and collected their luggage they were greeted by a tall, slim man in military uniform.

"Major Owens, it's been a while," said the man in a Liverpudlian accent.

"Ah, Sergeant Gibbs. Indeed it has. How are you this morning?" said Owens.

"I'm good thank-you, sir. How are you?" said Gibbs.

"Hanging in there. You know how it is, I never could sleep on planes. This is John Austin or Brooks as he will be known from now on," said Owens.

"A pleasure to meet you," said Gibbs and held out his hand.

"Thank you, and you," said John and shook the man's hand.

"If you would please follow me this way, gents, I will show you to your transport," said Gibbs.

John picked up Alex and the group walked into an open aircraft hangar. Vincent had already run ahead to escape the morning sun. Gibbs flipped a switch on the wall and large overhead lights flickered into life. Inside the hanger to their left was a long recreational vehicle. It looked as mundane as John had imagined it would from the diagrams.

"This here is your new home for the next few months, until we can get you back home," said Gibbs.

"What the hell? This thing is a wreck!" said Vincent.

"Don't worry, underneath it is extremely high tech," said Gibbs.

It was painted two tone, beige on the top half and brown on the bottom half. John walked around it looking at all the details. He knew from his experience as a mechanic that it looked about fifteen years old with some rusting on the wheel arches and a couple of scrapes here and there.

"What about all this damage? I thought it was new," he said to Gibbs.

"All the damage and aging is on the exterior is artificial. This is one tough cookie. It will take all small arms fire, some heavy artillery fire, and close quarters grenade dispersals," said Gibbs.

"What if they have something bigger?" said Vincent.

"This vehicle is designed to run. If they come at you with some high explosives you can haul arse out of there. It's no Lamborghini but it will give any sports car a run for its money," said Gibbs.

"What are we talking speed-wise," said John.

"0-60 in 5.2 seconds and a top speed of 160 mph in a straight line. I know it sounds crazy for a vehicle this size but I built and tested it myself. It has an engine four times the BHP and capacity of the vehicle it's based on. It can put most of that power down too. If you need to push or pull something this vehicle is more than capable," said Gibbs.

"That's incredible. How did you manage to fit an engine like that into a vehicle like this?" said John.

"I have a few tricks up my sleeve," said Gibbs with a smile as he tapped the side of his nose.

"Can we have a look round inside?" said John.

"Of course," said Gibbs as he fished the keys from his pocket and unlocked the side door. "After you, lads." When they were all inside Gibbs gave them a quick tour.

"You have a kitchenette, all the cutlery, pots, pans and, utensils you could need. Along the corridor the two doors on the left and two at the end are single bedrooms, the two doors to the right are the shower room and the toilet. I'll let you fight it out among yourselves as to who gets which room. The front is obviously where you drive this beast, but this is where the fun starts," said Gibbs.

He slapped his hand against the wall that separated the driver's area from the living area and a panel slid aside. In what had looked like a solid wall sat a rack of hand guns set back snuggly into the wall and numerous magazines of ammunition.

"All the ammo is ready to go. All you need to do is slide in a mag and choose your targets. We didn't want you to be caught out. Eventually, you will need to replenish the bullets but you should be good for a long while," said Gibbs with smug a smile.

"Cool," said Vincent.

John looked at his son with an amused smile.

"Well, that's it. All that is left is to give you these," said Gibbs as he handed the keys to Owens. "Goodbye for now and good luck."

"Thank you," said John and Owens.

Vincent smiled and Alex waved his little hand. Gibbs stepped out of the RV and closed the door. Vincent helped Alex into his child seat and fastened his belt before he and John took their seats. Owens sat in the driver's seat and slid the key into the ignition. It roared into life as he started it up.

"Will you listen to that," said John.

Owens looked back at him with a huge childish grin. He then drove the vehicle out of the hanger. Gibbs waved them off as they drove out of the airbase and into the French countryside.

Chapter 15.

They spent months travelling through France from town to town. Taking in the French culture while Vincent and Owens taught John how to speak French. He picked up enough to be able to cope in small conversations but would get lost if things got more complex. Alex began to pick up some words too. The summer was beautiful as they travelled through Toulouse, Vincent took an interest in the local female population and as a result John became more cautious in how much free time he allowed Vincent to have. They would camp further away from the towns but still in campsites so they weren't out of place. They started the night watches earlier and made sure to be on their way as soon as first light broke. This annoyed Vincent and the respect between him and his father grew fragile. As time progressed he knew this respect would soon reach a breaking point; John knew this too.

Soon months became a year. Their lives played out as normal as they could, given the situation they were in. John and Owens had discussed Vincent taking responsibility for a shift of the night watch and decided that he should take the two-hour shift between 12 am and 2 am.

It was midsummer and the nights were warm and humid. John had finished his shift at 12 and Vincent had taken over. It was an uneventful night and Owens came out to take over from him. He opened the door of the motorhome but kept an eye on the older man. As the Owens turned his back on Vincent he closed the door and used his vampire abilities to slip away.

He just needed to be free for a while, to be on his own. He was getting older, his hormones had kicked in and he was growing at an incredible rate. He stood six feet tall, with broad shoulders and shoulder-length brown hair. His limbs had bulked up and instead of looking like a gangly, awkwardly tall teenager he looked like a young man. He had an urge to run, to stretch his legs, and to use his body that had grown so much in the past year.

He stepped into an open field. He lifted one foot off the ground and rotated his ankle. He did the same with the other then set off running. He leapt over fences and dodged cows and goats as he sped through the darkness. He pushed himself harder and his hair whipped behind him as he picked up speed. He hurtled across field after field until he saw a building in his path. As he approached it at an enormous speed there was no time to dodge to either side. He squeezed his eyes shut and leapt as high as he could. He braced himself for the inevitable impact but it never happened. He opened his eyes and found himself soaring with ease over a barn. A smile played across his face but it was short lived as he realised he needed to land. He braced himself for the impact, hit the ground and was thrown forward. He rolled twice head over heels but then sprang back to his feet and continued running. He couldn't believe what had just happened. He laughed to himself and then out loud. He was having fun but realised he had to be cautious. He looked at his watch, nearly half an hour had gone and he needed to get back. He returned to the RV and slipped back in silently without alerting anyone.

His little act of rebellion was repeated over several

nights. After four days he was doing his usual running when he heard the roar of a motorcycle. He ran in the direction of the roar and got to the road just as the bike rode by. What he saw made his jaw drop. The rider was a young woman whose long black hair wisped behind her as she cruised by. Her pale, radiant skin seem to glow in the moonlight, and as her bright eyes met his a smile played across her pretty lips. Vincent watched her in awe and just about managed an awkward wave of his hand. She looked back, the smile still on her lips, and carried on riding. He just stood there, slack-jawed for a while, and watched her go. She was the most beautiful thing he had ever seen and as he snapped out of her spell he looked down at his watch. He saw that he was quarter of an hour later than he had planned for.

"Shit!" he said aloud.

He had to get back and fast. He slipped back into the RV just as John and Owens were changing shifts. He made the excuse that he had just got up to use the toilet. The next day seemed to take forever and that night he slipped away at the first moment that he got.

He circled the area and listened out for the girl's motorcycle. After fifteen minutes he heard it and ran to the road as fast as his legs could carry him. He stood and waited for what seemed like hours until he heard the roar of the engine. It grew closer and he saw her cruising up the road towards him. He stood by the side of the road and tried to play it cool; as if he just happened to be there. She looked at him and smiled that sweet smile…and continued to ride past. His heart sank as he watched her pass by. What happened next made it almost beat out of his chest. He heard the brakes squeak and the tires grind against the tarmac as the bike came to a halt. With a knee-length, heavy boot, that had more straps and buckles than were practical, she kicked out the stand. She then places the sole of that boot on the tarmac. As Vincent stood in awe she swung her other long, slender leg over the bike and turned to look at him.

"Hi stranger," she called to him in French.

"Good evening, madam," he said and prayed to everything holy that he would sound confident.

She smiled and looked him up and down.

"You're not from around here are you," she said.

"How can you tell?" he said.

"Your accent. Dead giveaway. Where do you call home, stranger?" she said.

"I'm from England. As you can hear my French needs a little bit of work. Do you speak English by any chance?" he said.

She smiled at him and cocked her head to the side a little.

"Yes I speak English, but you're French is better," she said.

To Vincent, her voice floated on the air like a feather on a summer breeze.

"We can continue in French if you like," he said.

"Yes please, your accent is so sexy," she purred.

"I'm…I'm Vincent…by the way," he said and tried with all his might not to stammer.

"Hello, Vincent. My name is Scarlett," she said.

"That a beautiful name," he said and felt the blood rush to his face.

"Thank you, Vincent. I like your name too. It is a strong name," she said.

She put her hands on her hips knowing that this would make him notice her hourglass figure. His eyes also noticed her tight leather pants that showed off her long, smooth thighs. Her outfit was topped off with a well-fitting biker jacket.

"That's a nice bike. What make and model is it?" he said in a vain attempt to make her think he wasn't looking at her body.

She smiled knowing that he was, and that she was checking him out too.

"It's a 1960 Triumph Bonneville," she said.

"Cool, with an overhead twin vertical engine block, 649cc, and about 46 bhp," he said, suddenly worrying that she might think he was a nerd.

"Yes, that's right," she said with a smile.

"Have you had the lower frame rail fitted to brace the backbone and steering head?" he said and smiled back.

"Yes. When I got the bike the modification was already done. I read that it makes the bike safer. How do you know so much about the motorcycle?" she said as she looked into his eyes.

"Oh I…er…don't really sleep much," he said.

He looked into her eyes and noticed they were an intense shade of blue.

"Me neither. Let me ask a question. You're are a vampire, yes?" she said.

"Er..." he said.

His mind began to grope for an answer but in this moment nothing he came up with seemed good enough.

"Don't Worry, Vincent, I can tell one of my own kind when I see them," she said.

"Yes, I'm a vampire. How can you tell?" he said.

"Besides, the fact that we are stood by an unlit road with only the moonlight for illumination? I can also smell it, I can see it in you. You see it in me too. Relax, Vincent. It's ok. You are new to this life?" she said.

"Yes, I was turned three years," he lied. Even though he was in awe of Scarlett he didn't know her yet and she was a vampire. He wasn't foolish enough to put his brother at risk because a woman had caught his eye.

"Aww, baby, you're so young. I remember it took me a long time to get used to being a vampire. How old were you before you were turned?" she said.

"I had just turned seventeen," he said.

"I was twenty. This is why I still look this way," she said as she pirouetted.

"And very beautiful you look too," said Vincent, thankful that his voice was steadier than his nerve.

"Aww, thank you, Vincent," she said with a smile. "Who turned you?"

"I didn't see them. I had been out with some friends and was walking down an alley on the way home. Someone attacked me from behind. When I came round my head was all fuzzy. I just put it down to the alcohol and continued to walk home. I didn't think about it and felt great until the sun came up and started burning my skin. I didn't know what was happening to me at first until I remembered the attack and realised it wasn't normal. That was 3 years ago."

"Aww poor baby. You must have been scared," she said with genuine sympathy in her voice. Her eyes widened and she let out a gasp. "You must have been turned by a first born!"

"A what?" he said playing into the lie.

"A first born'" she said.

But he still looked confused.

"A first born vampire. If you were bitten by a turned bitten vampire they would have to give you some of their blood in order for you to turn. If you're bitten by a first born you will turn from just that one bite. I was turned by a friend after I was caught in a bomb blast in World War 2. I was dying but she saved me and gave me a new life. She asked me before she did and I agreed. I didn't want to die at just twenty years old," she smiled at him. "Oh let me look at you, Vincent, you are so beautiful. I am so happy to meet a new friend," she said as she took his hand and turned him round on the spot. "Can I ask a private question?" she said.

"Er...yes, of course," he said.

"Have you fed on a human yet?" she said.

She asked in such a sweet way that it sounded like the most normal thing to do.

"No...I've...er...only fed on pigs," he said and looked sheepishly at the ground.

He felt ashamed that he might not stand up to her idea of what a vampire should be.

"Oh my. You are so young, so sweet. You must drink human blood, Vincent. The blood of the pig does not give all the strength you need," she said.

"I know, but I just feel so strange. I've got no one to help me with these things," he said.

"Well, Vincent, now you have me to help you," she said and smiled.

"I don't know, I just don't want to hurt people," he said.

"You are no longer a person. You are a big, strong vampire and so you must feed on strong blood," she said and placed her hands on his shoulders.

He was relieved by her reaction. He then looked into her eyes and started to realise he had lost track of time. He looked down at his watch and saw he had been here for 30 minutes.

"I'm sorry Scarlett, I'm going to have to go." He said.

"To where?" she said abruptly.

"I have to meet a friend," he said.

"Ok Vincent, but meet me here tomorrow?" she said.

"Yes, of course," he said

"Promise?" she said.

"Yes, I promise. I really need to..."

Before he could finish the sentence she grabbed him and pressed herself against him,

"I have many things to show you," she said then pressed her full lips against his and kissed him. "So many things."

"Ok," he said, his voice really was unsteady now.

He walked backward away from her with a big dumb smile all across his face.

"Tomorrow night, Vincent," she said and blew him a kiss.

"Tomorrow night," he said then turned and ran like the wind with joy in every step.

Scarlett climbed back onto her motorcycle, kicked the stand up and rode off into the night with a smile on her face.

He arrived back at the campsite just as John and Owens were changing shifts.

"Hello, son. Where have you been?" said John.

"I just went to the campsite toilet," he said thinking on his feet.

"Why? We have a perfectly good toilet in the Motorhome," said Owens.

"Yes, but it was a number two. I didn't want to stink out the RV." Said Vincent.

"Ok son," said John and laughed.

Owens however was not so easily convinced. He had seen vampires lie before. They were good at it but like any con artist, no matter how good, there are still had tells that gave them away. For now he decided to hold his tongue and see how things played out.

Vincent stepped inside the motorhome, put in his earphones, and got into bed. Not that he was going to get much sleep. Scarlett was the only thing on his mind and that was perfectly fine by him.

That night and the next day passed so slowly that Vincent could feel the passage of every single second. He hated the day. Having to stay inside all the time wasn't fun for a young vampire. Again Scarlett came into his mind, she was so beautiful. He had never been kissed before last night and like any teenager in his position he was love-struck. He couldn't wait for the sun to set and bring with it the glorious night.

As the RV bumped and bobbed along a French country road he moaned and groaned while he and John played the board game, Battleships.

"I hate the day," he said with a frown on his face.

"It's not that bad, I know what you mean though. It is boring being cooped up in here all day but it's not for that long," said John.

"It's ok for you, if we stop you can get out and have a

walk around and stretch your legs. I'm just stuck in here all the time."

"Are you sure you've not been sneaking out at night?" John said in a playful tone.

"No…No! Where would I go? What would I do?" said Vincent as he quickly stood up from the table.

"I'm only teasing you, Vincent. Come on sit down. Let's just play the game."

"Ok," he said and sat back down.

The day passed and the sun finally descended towards the horizon. When Alex and Owens had gone to bed Vincent saw his chance. He snuck towards the door when it swung open to reveal John stood there.

"Where are you going?" he said.

"Can I not go to the toilet anymore without you asking me a million questions," spat Vincent.

"Excuse me? Don't talk to me like that! Why are you so angry?" said John.

"I'm sorry Dad. It just feels like everyone keeps asking me where I'm going and what I'm doing all the time. I'm sorry," he said.

John's face relaxed and softened.

"Ok, just reign in that anger a bit. I was your age once, I know what it's like to be a teenager," he said then looked at Vincent with a sad smile.

"What?" Vincent said.

"I can't believe how big you are now. You're nearly a fully grown man. I never thought you would have grown up so fast. Your Mum would be so proud," he said as tears welled in his eyes.

Tears welled up in Vincent's eyes too. "I know. I wish I could have known her," he said

"I do too," said John wiping his eyes. "You should go."

Vincent smiled at him and walked into the night. At the first possible moment he ran as fast as he was able and got to the road in minutes.

Scarlett's bike slowed to a standstill, she kicked down the stand and smiled at Vincent. He smiled back at her and then walked over to her. She climbed off her motorcycle, wrapped her arms around his waist and planted a kiss on his lips.

"Hello, my darling. How are you?" she said.

"All the better for seeing you. How are you?" he said.

"I am wonderful, my dear. I have brought some friends to meet you. I hope you don't mind," she said.

Vincent's heart skipped with a hint of worry, but he quickly relaxed. He knew if he was going out into the world he would have to meet new vampires. He told himself this was a good thing. "No, that's fine," he said. That didn't stop the unease he felt as eight bikes pulled up behind Scarlett's. There were three Harley-Davidsons, three more Triumphs and two Kawasakis.

The vampire on the first Harley stepped off his bike and walked over to them.

"So this is the guy you were telling us about?" he said in a gruff Italian accent that had faded with many years of living in France.

He walked over and offered out his hand. Vincent reached out and shook it in a firm but friendly manner.

"I am Odio," said the vampire.

He was 5 feet 10, with a medium build, long greying hair and pale blue eyes. He looked to be in his early forties but he seemed much older in his mannerisms and the way he carried himself.

"Scarlett has told us many things about you," he said and smiled, showing off a long pair of white fangs.

"Really?" said Vincent with a smile.

"Yes, she told us all this morning about this new vampire she has met. Bitten by a firstborn vampire she said. Well, we found that to be of much interest," said Odio.

"Yes, a firstborn, a firstborn, a firstborn. Many times she has told us," said a seven foot tall, large built vampire as he walked up and stood next to Odio. His long blonde hair blew in the cool night breeze as he smiled at Vincent. "I am Reus, some people call me Giant. Usually while they're running away and screaming."

"Hello Reus," said Vincent with a smile.
All the vampires had gotten off their bikes and were stood around Vincent. Odio pointed to each of them and introduced them.

"This big guy is Destructeur, the girl with red hair is Destine. Doom with the beard is English, one of your fellow countrymen. The twins, Gek with the spikey purple hair and Seraphim with the blonde deathawk. The guy with the wild hair is Wulf, the woman next to him with the dreadlocks is Murderoar. The huge guy with the Mohawk is Bestia. The tall slim guy is Slee and the Woman with the curves is Luna," he slapped a hand on Vincent's shoulder, "Everyone, this is our new friend Vincent."
From the group came calls of "Hello," and "Hi Vincent."

"Hello everyone," he said.
Odio could hear the nervous tension in his voice.

"Don't be nervous. A friend of Scarlett's is a friend of ours," he said with a friendly slap on Vincent's back.

"Come for a ride with us," said Scarlett to Vincent.

"Erm…I," he said.

"You wouldn't let a pretty girl down would you?" said Doom with a smile.

He looked at Scarlett who stuck her bottom lip out and fluttered her eyelashes at him. He looked back at Doom who copied Scarlett's expression.

"Ok, I'll come," he said with a laugh.

"Wonderful. You can ride with me," said Scarlett as she jumped excitedly.

All the vampires got back on their bikes.

"Climb on behind me," Scarlett said.

He did as she said and got onto the bike.

"Sit closer to me, put your hands around my waist and hold on tight, beautiful," she said.

She looked around at him with a little smile and kicked up the stand. She then gunned the engine and sped away along the dark road. The other vampires sped up and rode alongside them, howling and laughing as they went. Vincent loved it, he had never been on a motorbike until this moment. The speed and exhilaration were completely different than when he ran. Scarlett controlled the bike with such ease it seemed like an extension of her body. Her frame was small but her vampire strength gave her the power to make it look effortless.

Seraphim got to her feet and stood up on the back of Gek's bike. She arched her arms up at her sides like flapping wings. Her hair flowed out behind her as they sped through the cool night air. Gek then put her arms out too, both of them howled and laughed enjoying the danger as adrenaline rushed through their veins.

"Vincent! How do you feel?" yelled Odio as he rode up alongside Scarlett's bike.

"I feel awesome!" he yelled back.

"Scream it! Let the world hear you!" yelled Odio.

"I feel awesome!" screamed Vincent.

Scarlett and Odio howled like banshees. The rest of the vampires joined them in a wild chorus.

They rode for what seemed like just over an hour but soon the first rays of sunlight illuminated the clouds on the horizon. They all slowed down as they came to an old dilapidated farmhouse. It was three storeys high, the roof bowed deeply in the middle and there was a big hole where some of the slates had fallen in. The front wall was covered in ivy so thick that from the road it was almost invisible amongst the overgrown garden and trees. They pulled into the muddy driveway and rode their bikes to the back of the house. All the members of the gang stepped off their bikes then headed in through the back door and then down the stairs to the basement. Vincent stood outside unsure of what to do.

"We have to get inside," said Scarlett as she pulled him by the hand.

He knew he had messed up and stumbled over his words.

"I...um...I should get back. My parents are waiting for me. They'll be angry if I...."

"Please stay with us. It is too dangerous to try and get back now. The sun will be up in the next ten minutes," she pleaded.

"It'll be ok, Vincent. We'll take you back when the sun sets again. Tell your parents you got up early and went out," said Odio.

His voice had a calming effect so potent that Vincent felt like a child being spoken to by a trusted grandparent. He was instantly relaxed and everything seemed like it was going to be ok.

"Ok. I'll stay," said Vincent.

"Come with me now, away from the sun. We have to get into the basement," said Scarlett.

He let her lead him into the house and down the stairs. The basement was almost the same length and width as the house. Some supporting walls divided the space and created one large main room with a smaller one at each end. In the large room there were mattresses, some old tables, and chairs. An underlying musty smell made Vincent crinkle his nose, and damp climbed the walls in patches. There was another smell too, one he couldn't quite place.

"Do you own this place?" he asked.

"My parents built the house…but that was nearly two hundred years ago," said Destructeur who was now sitting on an old sofa in the corner.

"So you have always lived here?" said Vincent.

"Well, no, we took it back in 1956," said Destructeur.

"Took it back?" said Vincent.

"Yes. Some humans were living here, but we took care of them," said Destructeur with an evil smile.

"We move around a lot. We have safe-houses, like this one, everywhere that we travel to at random. If any humans become aware of our feeding patterns we move to another property," said Odio.

"Sometimes there are what humans call squatters living in our safe-houses. It's always nice to have a warm meal waiting for you when you arrive at a safe-house," said Destructeur with that evil with an evil smile.

"Oh yes," Scarlett said suddenly. "Vincent has not fed from a human yet."

"Really?" said Odio.

"Yes," said Vincent with a sigh as his face reddened.

"Do not be ashamed my friend. We all have to start somewhere," said Odio. "Let us correct that right now," said Odio.

The blood drained from Vincent's face as he realised what that other smell was.

"Bring one of them out. A young, pretty one for our strong, young friend," said Odio in a jovial voice

"Wait, hold on," said Vincent.

Bestia disappeared down a corridor. A few moments later muffled screams came from the room he had entered. The vampires cheered as they surrounded Vincent and placed a chair infront of him. They moved aside as Bestia came through with a struggling package over his shoulder. He placed it down on the chair. A pang of horror raised in Vincent's chest as he realised it was a woman who he reckoned to be around the age of twenty. She was wrapped from her ankles all the way up to her shoulders in a cocoon-like layer of silver duct tape. More tape was also tightly wrapped around her head and covered her eyes and mouth. Only her nose was visible. She writhed and struggled as much as the tape would allow.

"Drink, drink, drink," chanted the group.

"Drink, Vincent. The first taste is as sweet as honey," said Odio.

"Drink, my love. It will make you strong," said Scarlett with her hands resting on his shoulders.

"Do not be afraid of what you are. You're purpose is to drink human blood," said Odio in that calm evoking voice.

"Drink her for me," said Scarlett in a sensuous tone. Vincent leaned over and place one hand on the side of the woman's head. She quivered with fright and her nostril flared as she let out a muffled cry. He looked at the other vampires then moved his face to her neck. He could feel the heat coming off her.

"Drink. Drink. Drink!" the vampires continued to chant.

He could see the blood as it pumped through the arteries and veins under her skin. He opened his mouth to reveal his long, sharp fangs. Every part of his body ached for this, then instinct took over as he thrust his teeth into her flesh. As he bit deep into her carotid artery the blood hit the back of his throat. He gulped it down and quenched the deep thirst that had always screamed in the back of his mind. It tasted amazing, every part of his body felt stronger and more powerful. The woman's cries turned to a gurgle, then stopped as she became limp. The blood stopped flowing with the cease of her heartbeat. Vincent tried to suck out more blood but there was no more to be had.

"It's done," he said.

Scarlett pulled him back and Odio slashed the other side of the woman's neck with his thumbnail, her veins were empty.

"By the gods! You drank her dry," he said with a little laugh. "I have lived more than seven hundred years and I have never seen a human drank dry so fast. You must have had one hell of a thirst my young friend."

"Vincent the fully fledged vampire!" sang Scarlett. The other vampires slapped him on the back and hugged him as the body was carried away. Vincent watched as they took her, he had expected to feel guilt at the taking of a life but found he did not care for her; not one bit. Scarlett grabbed him and kissed him on the mouth. She licked the remnants of the blood from his lips.

"Do not worry my love. The first time can be difficult but you are not human anymore. You are a strong vampire, a predator, but not a monster. We are merely higher on the food chain than them. Feeding on them is what we do. Be proud of what you are," she said.

"I am," he said and kissed her.

"Well done, Vincent. Welcome to your new life," said Odio and held out his arms. "This world is ours to take, so take it we must."

Vincent looked down at his hands he could feel the power and energy that rushed through him. It was an incredible sensation.

"This is amazing, I feel so strong," he said.

"It is a good feeling, yes. Now, there are some things you need to remember. One, after you have fed you will need to dispose of the body. There are many ways to do that. Burial or fire work well also certain acids will break up a body but they are hard to come by and dangerous to use. In the countryside we can bury the bodies or leave them out for wild animals to eat. In a city you can dump a body in an alley or an abandoned building is better. It might not be found for years in there," said Scarlett.

"What will happen to her body?" said Vincent.

"There is the air shaft from an abandoned mine in the land at the back of this farm. We throw them in there. It's over four hundred feet deep and the main shaft collapsed decades ago. No one goes down there anymore so they will never be found.

Two, never turn someone you do not like into a vampire. Not only are we difficult to kill but some vampire clans look down on vampires killing other vampires. The main reason is you don't want to have to spend the rest of time with some arsehole you don't like. Three, stay away from large groups of humans, a few can be easily killed but large groups will have an advantage over you."

"Safety in numbers, right?" said Vincent.

"Exactly," said Odio. "The main reason we live this nomadic lifestyle is because most humans don't believe in us anymore. They think we're just stories in movies and books. If they ever find out that we vampires are real there would be uproar and riots in the streets. When I was young I had friends who got reckless and thought the humans would fear them. They were killed by mobs of villagers. When the villagers told other humans they believed them. These stories were then passed between villages and towns and down through the families. Soon we became old wives tales, folklore, and myths. Even though humans don't believe in us anymore the doubt is still there in their minds. Most humans are still a little bit scared of the dark because without the light they can't see. And instinctively they know there are things that might be using the dark as camouflage. If a large group of humans were to see you attack someone they will gang up on you. One lion can take down a buffalo calf, but if the buffalo group together they could easily kill the lion. The point is humans are the same. In a large enough group they can kill you, so be careful. Stick to the shadows, and only take on lone humans or small groups."

Vincent nodded to acknowledge he was taking in the information.

At that moment music blared out of a stereo. Luna, Gek, Murderoar, and Destin came over. They danced and jumped around as they approached.

"Come on Vincent, dance with us. Don't let Odio bore you all night. You have centuries to fill with conversation, today we dance and sing," said Luna. "And maybe other things." She whispered in Scarlett's ear.

She flashed a look at Vincent and then back to Scarlett to who she gave a wink. Scarlett's cheeks blushed and she smiled shyly.

Odio furrowed his eyebrows at Luna but soon his expression softened into a smile as she danced over to him. She placed her arms around his neck and kissed his lips. Without taking his eyes off Luna Odio spoke to Vincent.

"Yes, dance, drink and have fun. We can talk another time," he said.

Vincent smiled then held out his hand and Scarlett took it. He pulled her towards him and she pressed her body against his and he kissed her.

The rest of the day was filled with dance and song and soon the sun began to sink towards the horizon again.

Chapter 16.

"Ok Vincent, I said I would take you home when the moon rose. Let me know when you're ready and I'll take you," said Odio.

"Ok," said Vincent as he stood up from the sofa he had been sitting on with Scarlett.

"Aww, I don't want you to go," she said and gave him a tight hug.

"I'll be back soon, I promise," he said and kissed her on the top of the head.

"Ok," she said as she pushed her lips into a pout. Odio pulled his jacket on and slapped Vincent on the back.

"Come on, lover boy," he said.

Vincent gave Scarlett another tight hug and kissed her lips. He and Odio then made their way outside and got on Odio's bike. He kick started the engine and kicked up the stand.

"Ready?" said Odio.

"Yep," said Vincent.

Odio opened the throttle and the bike kicked up a plume of mud as they sped up the path. They got onto the road and returned back to the spot where they had all met the night before. Odio pulled the bike up at the side of the road and Vincent climbed off.

"Ok dude, if you need any help just come back to the house. You remember the way?" he said.

"Yes, I remember. Thank you, Odio," said Vincent.

"If you need help with anything, just ask. You are part

of our family now. We'll look out for you," said Odio.

"Ok, I'll see you soon," said Vincent.

"Yes you will," said Odio with a smile. "Scarlett really likes you, she is like a sister to me. Don't let her down."

"I won't," said Vincent with a smile.

Odio revved the engine, opened the throttle just enough to spin the back wheel and spun the bike around one-hundred and eighty degrees on the road. He then shot off into the night, threw his fist up over his head and howled.

Vincent smiled and raised his fist into the air too. He then made his way back to the motorhome, on the way he thought about the event of the past twenty-four hours. He had tasted human blood and no matter what he did from this point on him and his life were changed forever. To his dismay John and Owens were both waiting for him when he approached the vehicle.

"Where the hell have you been!?" said John sternly.

"I got up early and went out," said Vincent in a flippant tone.

"Don't bullshit me, son. I'm not fuckin' stupid," spat John. He closed his eyes trying to control his temper. "You were out all last night and all today. Andra said to stay together, told us not to draw attention to ourselves. You must have been somewhere."

"I'm betting with someone too," said Owens.

"She also said we wouldn't be here long and that turned out to be a load of bollocks!" said Vincent.

"Don't take that tone with me. Do not take that tone with me!" said John as his voice broke into a bark."

"I've not done anything wrong," said Vincent.

"You been out all day and not let us know where you

were. We were worried sick about you!" said John.

"I just needed to get out. I can't stay cooped up in a motorhome all day. This might work for you but I can't do it… I can't do this anymore," said Vincent.

"You put us all at risk! You put Alex at risk! You can't do that. You know what he means to the world," said John.

"Oh yes. Alex, Alex, Alex. He's the only one you give a fuck about!" said Vincent.

"That's not true and you know it. We care about you just as much as we care about him," said John.

"Yeah whatever, you don't care about me. You only care about Alex because he's, what? 'The chosen one?' 'The end of the vampires?' I'm a fucking vampire! How do you think that makes me feel? I'm a vampire, dad!" said Vincent.

"Vincent, it's not like that," said John.

"Andra said this would happen," said Owens.

"So? What do you mean by that?" snapped John.

"I mean, he is going to leave us eventually. We won't be able to stop him if he wants to go," said Owens in a stern tone.

"Are you telling me how to raise my children?"

"No, I'm just telling you the facts, John. Eventually, he will want to go and be with his own kind. I won't be able to stop him when he does, I'm fifty-eight, John. He's a strong young vampire, he should be with his own people." Said Owens.

"Why the hell are you suddenly so eager for him to leave?" John said as he turned and stared Owens in the eyes. "I'm not asking him to go, I'm asking him where the hell he has been all night and day."

As he said the last sentence he pointed a finger at Vincent.

"I was out, ok old man. I was out." Spat Vincent.

"We already know that! Where is out? And don't you bloody dare call me old," said John.

Vincent looked away from John and sighed.

"Where is out!" said John in a sterner tone.

Vincent looked at John and smirked.

"Enough of your attitude! Where…Is…Out?!" said John getting more irate by the second.

"You're pathetic, you know that? You treat me like a child, I'm nearly fully grown but you think you can tell me what to do?! You're nothing but a pathetic human," said Vincent.

"Don't talk to your father like that, young man!" snarled Owens.

"Shut your fucking mouth you old fart. You can't tell me what to do either. I could destroy you like that!" said Vincent with a snap of his fingers.

He took a step towards Owens but John stepped infront of him and put his hand on his chest.

"Don't you even dare!" he said and pushed him away. Vincent stumbled a little but caught his balance. He walked with menace towards John. Owens lunged forward to grab Vincent but was knocked to the floor by a well-placed punch. Vincent shot out his hands towards John but a double punch to the face and sternum stopped him in his tracks. He used his speed and strength to grab his dad and pull him close.

"You really want to know where I've been? I've been out with a group of vampires. We partied, we danced and I drank human blood for the first time. I was just being what I am for the first time in my life, and you know what? I loved it. Human blood is so much more powerful than disgusting pig blood. It's sweeter, stronger, and makes me more powerful. I can still feel it rushing through my veins. You would have had me drink that foul swine crap for the rest of my life if it was up to you. Oh, while I'm telling truths, I found the letter from Andra. You know, the one you tried to burn. The one that says you don't have to look after me. The 'he is strong and can fend for himself' but you must look after oh so precious Alex. Yeah, that letter!" said Vincent.

"If you read it all you would know that she also said to look after you," said John.

"Bullshit, I've had enough of all this fucking bullshit! She said we would only be here temporarily! How long has it been, John? One year and three months, without any contact of any kind! That's not temporary, she abandoned us!" said Vincent.

"No, Vincent. No she has not!" said John.

"Yes she has, but you're too blind to see it. She abandoned you with a firstborn vampire and an old man who can't even take a punch as Alex's protectors! You can't even stop me, how would you stop a horde of vampires?" said Vincent.

"You're my son. I can't stop you because I have to hope that you are different. You're all I've got left of Annabelle, of your mother," said John in an attempt to appeal to Vincent's softer side.

"Not anymore. You can't hold the memory of my dead mother over my head anymore," said Vincent and dropped John to the floor. "I'm done with you, all of you. I'm out of here. I have a new family now, a family that understands me."

He stood in the cool night air and looked down on John as he lay on the ground. John thought he saw a look of sadness in his son's eyes, or maybe it was pity.

Whatever it was there was no doubt now that things had changed between them. Vincent then turned and ran into the darkness. After a few moments John heaved himself to his feet and stood up. He then helped Owens to get to his feet too. The old man stumbled slightly but regained his balance.

"Are you ok?" said John.

"Yeah," said Owens rubbing his jaw. "He just caught me by surprise. I forgot how fast they can be."

"I'm sorry for shouting at you," said John.

"No, you had every right to. I was undermining your authority," said Owens.

John smiled and slapped Owens on the back.

"I still shouldn't have shouted. It was a loss of control on my part."

"It's ok, honestly. I'm sure he will be back soon," said Owens.

Chapter 17.

Vincent made his way back to the farmhouse. When he got there an eerie quiet hung over the building. He began to panic. What if he had, as far as he knew, destroyed his relationship with his human family only to come here and his newfound friends had left without him? As he made his way round to the back his panic dissipated when he saw that all the bikes were gone with the exception of one, a Triumph. He made his way inside and down into the basement hoping that she would be there. His heart thumped a rapid beat as he found that all the other vampires were out except Scarlett.

She skipped towards him and welcomed him by jumping into his arms and they shared a deep passionate kiss.

"What are you doing here? I wasn't expecting you to return so early," she said.

"I got back and my parents shouted at me. They treat me like a little kid. So we argued and I just walked away," he said.

"Good for you, Vincent. I'm happy you're back."

"Where is everyone?" He said.

"They're all out hunting. They will probably be out till dawn," she said.

"Really?" he said and raised an eyebrow.

"M-hm," she said and snuggled against him.

They lay down on a mattress and talked for hours getting to know each other in the ways that only come with talking to someone one on one. Eventually, the questions turned to past lovers and unburdened talk of sex and romance.

"Have you ever been with anyone?" she said to him in a soft but matter of fact way.

"What do you mean?" he said.

"I mean sex. Have you ever made love to someone?" she said.

He looked shocked and quietly looked away.

"No," he said eventually.

She placed her fingers under his chin and turned his face up to look at her.

"You do not have to be ashamed, my Vincent. Sharing yourself with someone is an intimate act. It's not something that should be given easily. You are still young, do not be sad," she said.

"Can I er... can we... you know…have sex?" he said, nervously stumbling over his words.

She smiled at him so sweetly and he knew and he was falling in love with her.

"Yes, my Vincent, I was hoping you would ask. I will lead you, ok. First of all relax, this is supposed to be fun and nice so let go of your worries. Ok now, take off your clothing," she said.

He breathed out and tried to relax then stood up and removed his shirt. He hopped around as he pull off his jeans. After a few clumsy moments he stood there naked.

"Now lie down," she said.

He dropped back down to the mattress next to her and propped himself up on his elbows. She stood up and slipped off her t-shirt. She unbuttoned her pants then slowly slid them over her hips and down over the curve of her thighs. She turned her back to him, unfastened her bra and slid it down her arms. She turned to face him again and with one arm covering her breasts she threw the bra at him with her free hand. It landed on his chest. He picked it up and he could feel that he was ready; she could see that he was ready too. He looked at her, she was the most beautiful thing in the world to him. She slid off her knickers and stepped out of them.

"Are you ready?" she said.

"Hell yes!" he said and realised he sounded a little overeager.

She stepped onto the mattress and gracefully sat down over him and pushed him down again the mattress and kissed him. She moved down his body while she kissed and lightly flicked her tongue over his skin as she went. Each movement of her mouth sent shivers of pleasure through his body. She moved back up to his face and kissed his mouth.

"Your turn. Ok, kiss me here," she said and pointed to her lips and he kissed her mouth softly.

"Now here," she said and pointed her neck.
He kissed her.

"Now here," she said and pointed to her nipple.
He did as she asked. She pushed him back down and climbed on top of him.

"Ready?"

"Uh-huh," was all he could manage.

Half an hour passed and they lay together panting. She moved and lay her head on his chest, she brushed her fingers over his abdomen as they spoke about the things they had seen and people they had known. She did more talking than him but he made up some anecdotes, used storylines he had read in books, and placed himself in other people's stories. He felt bad for lying to her but the truth would ruin everything.

They got dressed and drank blood from another one of the bound humans as they needed to get their energy back. The rumble of engines filled the air as the others pulled up outside and soon they all filed into the house. Each one of them carried at least one taped up human.

"Wow, you certainly had fun tonight," said Scarlett.

"We got talking to this group of men and women in a nightclub. Odio did his glamour thing on them and made them think we were some famous rock band. After that it was easy pickings," said Wulf.

"Put them with the others," said Odio. They all took turns to make their way into the other room to lay down the cocooned victims. All of them cried and tried to call out but made nothing more than muffled, mumbling sounds. The vampires just laughed and mocked them.

"Vincent, you have returned," said Odio.

"Yes. My parents gave me shit about being out all night. We argued and I walked out. Fuck them, I'm not going back!" said Vincent.

"And I won't make you. You are one of us now, you are free," said Odio as a mischievous smile played across his face. "And you have become intimately accustomed with Scarlett while we were out." Vincent's jaw dropped and he blushed as much as a vampire can.

"How can you tell?" said Vincent.

"I can tell by your blood flushed cheeks, the smell, but mostly by the huge fucking smile on your face," laughed Odio.

Scarlett hugged Vincent,

"We are in love, Odio," she said.

"I know, my sweet. This is a time for a celebration! Bring a human and some glasses!"

Reus went back down the corridor and picked one of the humans while Doom brought the glasses. Reus slashed the man's throat and poured out 14 glasses of blood. Slee took the man and finished him off then threw his body aside.

"Raise your glasses high for today our family has grown by one. Vincent is our new brother and the lover of Scarlett!" bellowed Odio.

All the other vampires cheered and drank their glass of blood.

For the first time in his life, Vincent felt happy and felt like he belonged. He loved his new family. In their time together they taught him things that no human could even begin to understand. How to hunt with speed and stealth in a way no human could. To feel the night and the air in ways no human had a need for. He loved to feed, he loved the strength and the mindfulness that it gave him. Most of all he loved Scarlett. He was content and time passed with ease.

Chapter 18.

10th October 1998.

The air had grown cold and the trees had begun to drop their leaves as autumn set in. After nearly four weeks John's hope started to fade and he had to give himself up the truth that he may never see Vincent again. Despite this, he would never stop looking for him. He and Owens stood talking at the side of the motorhome.

"We're gonna have to keep moving," said Owens.

"I know," replied John as a sad expression settled on his face. "I don't want to lose Vincent, I know he's a vampire and everything but he's still my son. After Annabelle died I was left alone. My parents both died when I was in my teens and I'm an only child. Annabelle's mum and dad both died the night that Andra saved us. They had no other children either. It was just me and the kids but now I've gone and fucked that up too. I just hoped he wouldn't grow so quick."

"I don't mean to talk out of turn but Vincent can look after himself. He's a strong intelligent man. Despite what you might think you raised him well but he's a vampire. They just can't live in close proximity to us. We have to look after Alex. That is our mission now. That really was the mission from the start," said Owens and his mouth curled downward in an apologetic frown.

"Yep. At least I know he still needs me," said John. His mouth smiled but his eyes were sad.
Alex, who was now 4 years and 10 months old, threw a ball up in the air and caught it.

"Come on Alex, time to go," said John.

"What about Vincent," said Alex

"He is ok. We'll meet up with him later. So we're going to go now," said John.

"Ok," said Alex with a sigh and then ran into the motorhome.

They got everything packed up, put everything into its storage space and set off. They only made one stop that day to fill up on petrol and gas then they were on their way.

Chapter 19.

30th July 2003.

The last four years had passed slowly for Owens. He and John no longer got along as well as they had when all this started and Alex, who was now eight and a half years old, was a pain in the arse in Owens's opinion. The kid whined far too much for his liking. Every time they went into a shop to buy food and supplies he always wanted a new toy or something. Like the time he had thrown a DVD case down an aisle just because John said he couldn't have it. John had shouted at Alex but that was it.

"If he was my son he would have received a beating," Owens had said.

"Just as well that he's not your son then isn't it," John had replied.

"He needs to learn some respect. If you're not man enough to do it I will!" Owens had said as his rage burned in his chest.

"With that attitude I'm not surprised your kids don't want to know you anymore," John had said.
That had hurt Owens more than he had expected it to. Time was no longer on his side as his sixty-third birthday was approaching far quicker than he had ever prepared for. His wife, Jane, had died seven years ago in an automotive accident that had later been deemed as suicide. He missed her so much but was in no mood to join her any time soon. He missed his kids too, Kelly and Jason. They hadn't talked or come to visit him in years even before their mother had died. They blamed

him for their mother's death though he had always protested wasn't his fault. The army was a full-time career for him, it wasn't just something he could walk away from. She could have told him that she wasn't happy but she never even spoke to him about how she felt. She just let it build and build then one day when he was stationed halfway across the country something in her snapped. They expected him to take the blame but he was sick of taking the blame for other people's actions.

All these thoughts span around in his mind as he drove the motorhome. He looked down at his hands on the steering wheel. They were the hands of an old man.

'All these skills I've acquired. All my life I've given to this cause. They are all just going go to waste when I die? Andra sends me out here with these people I didn't even know back then. Vincent was right, she's abandoned us. I've given my life to the military and what have I even received in return? A specialised skill set that I can hardly use anymore, a dead wife and a family who hate me. Now I'm probably gonna die here old and alone. Why should the vampires live forever while I die? This dickhead speaks to me like he knows me, like he can relate to the things I've seen because he's had a bit of training. Well, bollocks to him and his arsehole sons. I need a plan.' He thought to himself.

"How's it going, Owens?" said John as he walked into the driver's cabin and sat next to him.

"Hmm? Oh, I'm ok. Just a little tired. How are you?" said Owens.

"I'm ok thanks," said John.

Alex shouted from the middle of the vehicle about playing with a new toy robot John had bought him. He stood up and left Owens with his thoughts again as he walked away to play with his son.

'That kid really winds me up. I thought this vampire killer would be like some saintly Jesus type. All he ever does is make noise and a mess. He's just a little shit. I would gladly take the vampires over him,' thought Owens.

At that moment the seed of an idea planted itself in his mind. It was small but it began to take shape over the next couple of days. In the meantime, they stopped, slept, and took watch. All the while Owens acted like there was nothing wrong but the idea kept building. One afternoon they were all outside the motorhome eating their lunch. Owens bit into a sandwich as he sat and seemed to be lost in a daydream.

'All my life I've watched humans kill humans in wars over stupid arguments. Over land, religion, and natural resources. I've never seen vampires start wars, or for that matter kill each other for petty reasons. I've been in wars with vampires but they only attack us because they feed on us. We kill them in an attempt to wipe them out. They only kill us to keep us from destroying their race. Maybe that's what they are. They're the homo-superior, the next step in human evolution and they're trying to keep us in line. If I could join them I could live forever. With my history though they're never going to just accept me. If I had something to give them to show that I was serious ' he thought to himself.

Alex was supposed to be eating too but instead he was complaining that he had lost his football. A shiver of anticipation run up Owens' spine and it pulled him out of his daydream.

'I already have all I need to give the vampires for them to accept me. If I give them Alex they will be able to stop him before he's able to fulfill the prophecy. Surely then they will have to accept me and turn me into a vampire. I will be superior to the bastards who have held me down for so long. I'll live forever, my body will be strong and stop aging,' he thought.

He smiled as his deceitful plan grew and corrupted his mind.

Two days later they drove past an old farmhouse that was renowned to be haunted. Some of the locals had told Owens, on a rare night off, that a couple who had lived there in the 1950s had mysteriously disappeared without a trace. According to the urban myths, anyone who went in the house was never seen again. Screams of the restless spirits could be heard at night at different times of the year. Owens hadn't believed the stories but now he saw the building for himself.

'A classic vampire hideout,' he thought.

He continued to drive past for another five minutes, then he began to put the first phase of his plan into action.

It was seven pm and dusk approached fast as the sun sunk towards the horizon. Everything was going well when he intentionally wrenched the steering wheel back and forth causing the motorhome to swerve. The whole vehicle swayed from side to side and the wheels screamed as they tried to maintain traction on the road. John and Alex screamed from the back. Owens slammed his foot on the brakes and brought the vehicle to a halt. John made sure Alex was ok and then ran into the driver's cabin.

"Owens, what happened, are you ok?" he said.

"There must have been an accident. Stones from the wall were all over the road. I tried to avoid them but they were all over the place. I think the tyres have been damaged. I'll go and check it out," said Owens.

"Ok, I'll come and help you," said John.

"No, you and Alex stay on board. It's getting late. There might be something out there. You're both safer in here," said Owens, thinking on his feet.

He opened the side door, stepped down to the road. and walked round to the right side of the motorhome. He smiled to himself, they both knew that the tyres were bulletproof but luckily John seemed to have forgotten and his trust in Owens had blinded his judgement. He opened a panel on the side of the motorhome that concealed a toolbox and sign that read 'Hydraulic Jacks'. Below it were two buttons, one was marked 'Lower' and the other marked 'Raise'. He placed his finger on the 'Lower' button, pushed it in and held it. Four hydraulically driven ram jacks, located in the inside corner of each wheel arch, lowered from the underside of the vehicle. The feet of the jacks planted solidly against the road and the motorhome was raised up by over a foot. The whole vehicle shuddered slightly as they reached their maximum height. He opened the toolbox, took out a crowbar and walked to the front right tyre. He forced the crowbar under the rim and with all his bodyweight he pushed down. The tyre burst over the wheel rim and the air escaped so fast the noise it made sounded nothing like a puncture. He forced the crowbar around the edge, lifting the rest of the outside edge of the tyre completely over the rim. He did the same with the rear right tyre. This ensured the vehicle was un-driveable. He threw the crowbar into the undergrowth along the side of the road and climbed back onto the motorhome.

"What's happened? What was the popping noise?" said John.

"It was the hydraulic Jack system regulating the pressure. Both the right-side tyres are off the rims. We don't have anything to fix them and there is no way we will be able to drive on them. However there is a town nearby, I'll go and find a Mechanic. You and Alex stay here, I'll be back in about half an hour," said Owens.

"We'll come with you," said John.

"No! It'll be dark soon. You're safer in here than walking into the town," said Owens.

"Ok," said John with a smile.

Owens stepped down out the motorhome, and started walking up the road. Phase one was complete, he now began phase two.

After walking for fifteen minutes he found the old farmhouse. The house and garden had fallen into disarray with broken windows, damaged masonry, and the garden was wildly overgrown. He could hear the faint sounds of laughter so he made his way around to the back of the building. There he found nine Motorbikes. He walked in through the open back door and located the basement door. He knocked on it and the house fell silent. He knocked again, harder this time.

"Hi, can you open the door, please! I know you're vampires and I know you can hear me. I…er…I come in peace with an offer that will save you and all you're vampire friends!" he said.

He winced at his own words. 'Vampire friends? Man, I sound so old,' he thought.

The door swung open fast and bounced against the wall. A tall man with long greying hair and pale blue eyes looked Owens up and down with a serious look of disdain.

"Hello, I come with an off..." Owens' voice was cut off as the vampire's hand wrapped around his throat and lifted him from the ground. The vampire then swung him around and slammed him against the wall.

"How the fuck do you know we're here? What do you mean by an offer that will save all vampires?" said Odio. His voice was a low hiss but his grip was too tight and Owens choked as he tried to draw breath. He looked around and dragged Owens through the door hole and pulled the door shut behind them. After being thrown down the basement stairs Owens landed in a heap on the floor. Odio strode down after him and hauled the man to his feet. The other vampires were beginning to crowd around them.

"Answer my fucking questions! How did you know we would be here and what is the offer of which you speak? Who are you with? The military? The police?" said Odio.

"I'm not from around here. I'm English," said Owens.

"No shit, Sherlock. You better start answering my questions or you, motherfucker, will not be leaving this place. Who are you with and how do you know we are vampires?" said Odio.

"I am a Major in the British Army. My name is Anthony Owens. In my time in the army I heard about a vampire hunting unit. From them I learnt about vampires and where they usually hideout, so I took an educated guess. I also learnt about the prophecy from them. Do you know of this?" said Owens, years of training kept his voice steady.

"Of course I know of the fucking prophecy! A Boy born of a pregnant human woman bitten by our Lord. The elders say this boy would destroy the vampire race, like an apocalypse. Every vampire knows this story. It's been passed down for millennia from the very first of our kind, Lord Ruhsarr. They say the beast that made him also cursed him. It's a myth, nothing more," said Odio.

"That's what I am here to tell you. It's true, all of it. The boy was born just over eight years ago and I know where he is," said Owens.

Odio eyed him with a great deal of suspicion.

"Why should we trust you, Owens?"

"I know it must be strange to have a human come here and tell you that the prophecy is all true but please trust me. I know where he is because I have been protecting him for the past four years. He is right here in France, just a little way up the road in fact," said Owens.

"You work for the vampire hunting unit?" said Odio, he furrowed his brow and bared his teeth as a wave of anger swept over him.

"No, no. I'm just helping to transport him," said Owens.

"So you would betray the boy you were assigned to protect and you expect me to trust you? You'll have to do better than that, Owens. Destructeur, Murderoar, go and check outside. If there is anyone out there kill them," said Odio.

He then began to tear at Owens' shirt. Owens tried to stop him but he was far too strong.

"What are you doing?!" said Owens.

"Are you recording all of this? Are you wearing a wire?" He clamped his hand around the Owens' throat. "How many of you are there?"

"Just me, please, I'm alone," croaked Owens. He threw Owens down and pressed his head against the floor with the sole of his boot.

"You have come here to kill us all!" said Odio in a snarl and pressed his foot down harder.

"No, please, I'm telling you the truth," said Owens.

"You expect me to walk my family into a fucking trap? Do you think I'm that stupid?" Owens could feel his skin grind against the concrete floor. He knew it would be no trouble for a vampire like Odio to crush his skull like an egg.

"Please, please. Don't kill me. I have turned my back on humanity. I give this information to you because you don't deserve to be wiped out. Humans have no right to kill vampires!" Owens cried out and his whole body shook with fear. Odio could tell by the shrill tone of Owens' voice that he was telling the truth. He lifted his foot from his head, took him by the shoulders and lifted him to his feet. He swept the muck from the sides of his head and dusted him off.

"Ok. So let's say we trust you and you give us this boy, what is in it for you?" said Odio.

"I want to be one of you?" said Owens.

"And why would you want to become a vampire, old man?" said Odio.

"I have lived for sixty-two years, my wife is dead, and my family hates me. I am a Major in the British Army, a career soldier and have been for forty-four years. I am trained to the highest standard in armed and unarmed combat but I am only human. One day I will die, all my skills will be lost and I don't want that. If you gave me the chance to be a superior being, like yourselves rather than just human, I would be a respectable, strong, and worthy ally of the vampire race," said Owens.

"Ok Owens, my name is Odio, and as you can tell I lead this family of vampires. I am going to give you the benefit of the doubt just this once. You listen to what I say, you do as you are told and you will survive this night. If you do not…well I suppose you can already imagine what will happen."

"Yes sir. I understand," said Owens.

Odio turned to Destin.

"Where are Vince and Scarlett?" he said.

"They're out hunting," she said.

"We'll wait for them to come back," said Odio.

"With respect, Odio, the boy is in a motorhome just under a mile away. He and his father are going to wonder where I am soon. We have to go as soon as possible. If they see what I have done to the vehicle they may become suspicious," said Owens.

"Ok, we only have one chance at this. You take us there, we'll kill the father and bring the boy back here alive. We'll contact our elders, and when we have confirmed that this is the correct boy only then will we make you. Do you hear me Mr. Owens?" said Odio.

"Yes sir, loud and clear," said Owens.

"Destine, you stay here. When Scarlett and Vince

return tell them we will be back soon. Ok, let's move. Owens, you ride with me and lead us to this boy," said Odio.

They all made their way outside and climbed on their bikes. They then rode around the house and sped off in the direction of the motorhome. Moments later Scarlett and Vincent arrived back at the house just in time to see all the bikes leaving. Not knowing that Destin was waiting for them to return they followed their friends.

In the motorhome John had become impatient. The sun had set and the darkness crept over the fields that surrounded them. He close the book he had been reading to Alex, stood up and kissed his forehead.

"Stay in bed now son. I'm just going to check outside," he said.

"Ok dad," said Alex.

He took a torch that hung from a hook next to the side entrance of the motorhome and stepped out into the cool night air. He walked around the vehicle looking at the Jacks and the wheels off their rims. He was about to go back inside when something in the undergrowth near the wall reflected the light from his torch. He bent down and reached into the grass and picked it up. As he looked at the object in his hand a sense of dread fell over him. This was the crowbar from the motorhome's toolkit. He ran over to one of the wheels and inspected the rim. He found that both the rim and the tyre bore scratch marks that matched the end of the crowbar perfectly. His heart beat harder in his chest as he realised what was had happened.

"Oh for fucks sake, Owens. You arsehole, you fucking

arsehole!" he said.

In his eight years as a car mechanic he had picked up some tips and tricks. His mind raced through them all as he tried in desperation to remember anything of use. To his relief the trick he needed popped into his mind. His friend had shown him a way to get a tyre back onto a rim in seconds.

He ran inside the motorhome and opened a cupboard next to the oven rifled through its contents. His hands shook both fear and anger as he took out a bottle of lighter fluid and the long oven-lighter. He ran back outside to the front wheel and steadied his hands as he somehow knew he would need to work fast. He sprayed the lighter fluid into the front tyre and set it alight. The resulting flame caused the gasses inside the tyre to expand and push it back onto the wheel rim with an audible 'pop'. He then did the same with the back tyre and pulled a hose from the same panel as the jack control. He attached it to the valve on the wheel, and an air compressor chugged into life. The tyre was fully inflated in few seconds. After the rear tyre was also inflated he pressed the 'Raise' button on the panel for the jacks. There was a hiss as they eased the vehicle back down to the road and returned to their default position. He closed the panel, got back onboard, and carried Alex to the driver's compartment. He sat him in the passenger seat and fastened his seatbelt.

"What's happening dad?" he said.

"We're moving on," said John.

Alex blinked then rubbed his eyes and looked around.

"Where is Mr. Owens?"

"We're going to go and meet him in the town he spoke

about," said John in an attempt the keep his son from becoming scared.

"But I thought we were supposed to wait for him?" said Alex.

"There's been a change of plan," said John and tried to keep his voice calm

He pulled his own set of motorhome keys from his pocket. He had had them cut two days after they had set off. He hadn't known Owens too well back then and had learnt many years ago not to trust people just because they made a good first impression. He slid the keys in the ignition, started the engine and drove away. He had no idea where to go he just knew he had to get away from here.

"I thought Mr. Owens said the tyres are damaged," said Alex.

"They were but I fixed them," said John.

"How?" said Alex.

"A trick a friend taught me a few years ago," said John.

"But…" said Alex.

"Alex, no more questions!" said John.

Alex's realised he was pushing his dad's patience and kept quiet as John weaved expertly along the winding country roads. In the four years of driving the vehicle he had gotten used to the way it handled.

Odio's bike screeched to a halt where Owens said the motorhome was and where, until a few moments ago, it had been. Odio climbed off the bike looking around. He threw out his arms, turned on his heels and stared at the old man who was seated on the back of his bike.

"What the fuck is this?" said Odio.

"It was here!" protested Owens.

"Well it's not here now!" said Odio.

"It was here I'm telling you. This is where I left it," said Owens.

The other vampires pulled up alongside them.

"What's going on?" said Destructeur.

"This human says he left the motorhome here. Do you see a motorhome?!" snarled Odio.

"Hold on. Do you smell that? It's like lighter fluid and exhaust fumes," said Bestia.

He and Wulf got off their bikes and started searching around sniffing the air.

"There are deep tyre marks in the mud here at the side of the road," said Wulf.

"There's more over here too. They set off at a hell of a speed," said Bestia.

"Quick, back on your bikes. We can catch them," said Odio.

They set off again in the direction as the motorhome had travelled. After a few minutes the motorhome came into view.

As they gained on John he heard the collective sound of their motorbikes engines. He looked in the side mirrors and in the light of the crescent moon he could make out the silhouettes of a few of them. He knew something wasn't right because none of their headlights were on. Something scraped along the left side of his vehicle so he put his foot down and sped away. Within seconds though the bikes were gaining on him again. He tried to keep a cool head but all the vampires began to scream and howl and gun their engines. He knew this

was an attempt to scare him into making a mistake.
Instead, he slammed on the brakes. The Motorhome slid
and weaved as the tyres ground against the tarmac. He
heard the screams of the vampires and the.crumpling of
metal as their bikes slammed into the back of the much
larger vehicle. Three of them managed to dodge around
the motorhome and ended up infront of him. A huge
vampire on one, two women with crazy hair on another,
and two men on the other. A vampire with long greying
hair and an old man. Not just any old man though. John
recognised Owens instantly and his heart sank.

"You fucking son of a bitch!" John shouted as he
stamped on the accelerator.
The motorhome swerved a little then the tyres found
purchase and he aimed all four tonnes of the vehicle at
Owens. Odio spun the bike around but the motorhome
clipped it and knocked them both off. Odio jumped
angrily to his feet and picked up the bike but the back
wheel was damaged beyond repair. At that moment
Vincent and Scarlett caught up with the group and
stopped their bikes.

"Reus, lend me your bike," he barked.
The big vampire strode off the vehicle without a word.

"We'll push him further along, you run ahead and hit
them," said Odio.
Reus nodded then jumped up over the wall at the side of
the road and ran.

"Are you all ok?" Odio said to the others who were
picking themselves and their bikes up off the floor.

"Yes, we're ok but some of our bikes are fucked," said
Murderoar.

"Ok. Double up, I need all of us on this," said Odio.

Owens got on the bike with Odio and they sped after the motorhome. Vincent kicked down the stand of his bike and climbed off.

"Here take mine," he said to Wulf.

"Are you sure?" said Wulf.

"Yes. I'm gonna help Reus," he said.

"You can ride with me," said Scarlett.

"No. You take Luna. I'll see you when we catch the motorhome," he said.

"Ok," she said.

Vincent smiled at her and jumped over the wall. As he ran after Reus all sorts of thoughts rushed through his head.

'I love my vampire family but that's my real family in the motorhome. I can't just let them kill my family…but if Alex survives he will kill all vampires; including me. If they don't kill him one day I might have to fight him myself. He's my brother, I can't just let them kill my brother; or my dad. Man, why does everything have to be so difficult?'

These thoughts tore through his mind like broken glass and he knew either way one of his families would die that night.

'I could reason with my vampires but that will mean revealing who I really am. Is knowing where Alex has been all this time and not telling any other vampires worthy of my death? If I fight for or against them I'm killing one of my families. If I walk away I'm killing my related family. If I fight against the vampires and kill them that is worthy of death, at least that's what Odio told me. I can't let them kill my human family, I just can't. They're not going to kill my family. John is my

Dad, he gave me life. Without him I wouldn't even be here. Even with Andra's training he can't take on thirteen vampires by himself. Vampire or not, what kind of person would that make me?'

He was struck by a sudden realisation. The true reason why his brother was human and he was a vampire. What is the best defence against a vampire but another vampire? His reason for being born was to protect his brother.

'I can't let them kill him. If Alex dies I have failed.' This realisation made him run faster than he ever had in his life.

Odio and the other vampires roared up behind the motorhome. John weaved the vehicle from side to side in an attempt to stop them from getting past. The vampires gunned their engines and screamed. All of John's attention was on the bikers when out of the darkness a huge shadow lunged over the wall and hit the motorhome from the right side. The impact threw the vehicle off balance and the whole thing went up on the two left wheels. Alex screamed as John tried in a panic to right the vehicle. The shadow had been Reus and he now ran alongside the motorhome. Blood poured from a cut along the top of his head as he had not expected the vehicle to be so solid. He looked up and saw it sway back and forth in an unstable manner. He reached up a hand and gave it a push on the underside. It didn't take much to throw the centre of gravity over too far. The motorhome leaned over and veered to the right. The front bumper caught the wall and sent lumps of stone cascading into the field. It crashed down onto the tarmac on its left side and slid. Inside everything appeared to happen in slow motion. The windshield crunched and spider-webbed but didn't shatter. Pots and pans fell from the cupboards and crashed in all directions. Alex and John screamed as their entire world swung and slammed violently to the left. To them the motorhome seemed to slide forever and outside Odio smiled.

"Reus, you are a fucking force of nature!" he said. Owens and all the vampires cheered. All except Vincent who crouched down out of sight behind the wall. Tears ran down his face.

Reus jumped up on the motorhome then grabbed the door handle and tried to open it but it was locked. He pulled the handle with more force and it came away from the door in his huge hand. So, he pounded his balled up fist against the edge of the door and eventually made a hole. He put his hand into it and pulled at the door. A flash of pain split across his hand and he stepped back with a growl. He looked down at his hand and all his fingers had been sliced off. He roared and thrust his other hand in and pulled the door so hard it was torn completely away from the vehicle. In a fit of rage he put his head down into the empty door-hole and roared. The barrel of a shotgun come out from the darkness and slid between his teeth and into his mouth. Reus' eyes widened as a finger squeezed the trigger. There was the crack of the shell dispelling and his head disappeared in a blast of ash and silver shot. The vampires gasped as the headless body reeled back and fell from the vehicle to the road. It then writhed as it burned up and crumbled into big chunks of ash.

"Reus! No!" screamed Odio.

They all stood in shocked silence for a moment that was

broken by Odio.

"Fucking kill them!" he said as his voice cracked into a roar.

Destructeur ran and leapt onto the motorhome. John climbed up onto the side of the vehicle then squatted down, aimed at him, and fired twice. The first shot took off Destructeur's leg and the second ripped his chest apart. The vampire burned as he fell to the ground where he shattered into ash and broken bones. John shot three more shots at the approaching vampires but they moved far too fast. He put down the shotgun, swung a Colt C7A2s from his shoulder, flicked off the safety and fired. Seraphim was hit in the chest and she fell to the ground. Gek grabbed her and dragged her over the wall out of the line of fire.

"You're ok, you're ok," said Gek with tears in her eyes.

"No I'm not," said Seraphim,

Flames burst from her chest then spread to the rest of her body and burned her to ash.

Gek convulsed with sobs.

"No! You bastard," she roared and leapt over the wall towards the motorhome.

Wulf leapt over the wall to avoid the gunfire and landed next to Vincent.

"Vincent… Why are you crying?" he said.

"Because, I have to do this," he said and punched Wulf in the face. Wulf reeled back as Vincent swung for him again but he managed to dodge the attack. He stepped forward and punched Vincent in the head. Vincent fell but managed to grab Wulf by the neck and pulled him to the ground. Wulf clawed at Vincent's face but he slammed Wulf's head against the ground and held it there. He punched his fist into Wulf's chest, grabbed his heart and tore out the still beating organ. He bowed his head as his friend's body writhed and burned to dust. He jumped over the wall, grabbed Slee from behind, and threw him to the ground. He then stood on the slim vampire's back, grabbed his head with both hands and pulled upwards. The soft tissue of Slee's neck stretched and then tore. The vertebrate and tendons snapped as his head broke away from his body. Vincent dropped the head as it and the body disintegrated into ash.

Gek leapt at John and kicked the gun from his hands. Quickly he pulled a katana from his back and swung it at her but she jumped over him. He spun around to face her as she landed and cut off her right arm as she swung it at him. She punched him in the ribs with her remaining arm then kicked him away. He looked up at her but she moved so fast that she appeared to vanish. He turn again and as he did he swung the sword. She was stood infront of him swaying slightly. Blood poured from her mouth, she dropped to her knees and fell in two at the chest.

The vampires attacked the motorhome in all at once now. John saw them coming and readied himself. Murderoar leapt at him, he dodged but was shoulder charged by Bestia. Doom hit him hard in the face, then Murderoar and Bestia kicked him in the ribs. He swung the sword and cut off both Murderoar's legs. She screamed in pain as she landed. Bestia punched John again but he grabbed the vampire by the hair and head-butted him in the face twice. Bestia reeled back as blood gushed from his nose. John jumped back to his feet, swung the sword and sliced off both Bestia's arms. He slid the sword back into its scabbard and drew two MP-443s from his hip holsters. He shot both Murderoar and Bestia multiple times in the chest. The two vampires writhed as they burned up. Doom grabbed John by the throat and threw him down to the road. Both Doom and Odio grabbed him and started to beat him. Doom kick John hard in the balls. He cried out and fired the guns at the two but they dodged the bullets. Odio knocked the gun from his right hand. It slide across the tarmac and was picked up by Owens. He looked at the gun then aimed it at Vincent who was running at Doom and Odio and pulled the trigger. The bullet zipped past Vincent's head as he grabbed Doom and pulled him away from his dad. Owens pulled the trigger again but bullets hit Doom who Vincent was now using as a shield. He ran at Owens and threw Doom. Owens flinched but was only hit by ash. Vincent's fist appeared through a cloud, hit Owens in the face and sent him sprawling across the ground. He then grabbed the old man by the head and slammed him it against the tarmac.

"You treacherous fuck! How could you do this to us, you bastard?!" he said and slammed Owens' head into the floor again. "You gave up my dad and my brother for what, for what you fucking arsehole?!"

"I wanted to be like you. I wanted to be a vampire," said Owens.

You traded us in?!" roared Vincent.
He gripped the old man's head in this hands and squeezed. Owens saw absolute hatred in the young vampire's eyes as his skull cracked and then collapsed. Vincent screamed his rage into what was left of the man's face.

Odio and Luna were fighting with John who was now on his feet. The two vampires were circling him like wolves as they waited for their prey to weaken. Luna strode towards him and he pointed the gun at her. She knocked it from his hand as he pulled the trigger and the bullet missed her by inches. She roared at him but he roundhouse kicked her in the face and blood spurt from her nose.

"Keep coming at me, I'll just keep breaking that nose of yours," he said in a hiss.

"You fucking arsehole!" she roared as she pulled her nose back into place.

Odio went in to attack and John swung his katana at him but missed. He grabbed John round the chest as Luna stepped in, and punched John in the face, breaking his nose.

"See how it feels, bitch!" she said with a smirk.

John swung the sword at her but she grabbed his arm and snapped his wrist. He clenched his teeth and cried out in pain. She grabbed his nose and twisted it causing him to howl.

"We're gonna take your boy," she said.

"Fuck you," he hissed as he cut her feet from under her.

Vincent appeared beside her in time to catch her by the knees and threw her into the underside of the motorhome. He then grabbed her by the neck and squeezed until he felt the bones break. She choked and raised her hands to her throat. He then thrust his hand into her chest and pulled out her heart. Her body was ash before it reached the ground.

"You piece of shit!" yelled Odio, his face twisted in

anger.

"Fuck off, you prick," said Vincent.

"Why are you protecting these people?" said Odio.

"Because they're my family!" said Vincent.

"Are you saying this man this man your father?" said Odio.

"Yes. I'm sorry. I can't just stand aside let you kill him," said Vincent.

"You lied to us! You said you were bitten," said Odio.

"My brother and I survived after our mum was bitten. I'm a born vampire with a human family. I can't let you kill them," said Vincent.

"We were your family, Vincent! We trusted you and you have killed us!" said Odio. He looked down at John and then up at Vincent. "You should say goodbye," said Odio.

He held John by his shoulders and forced him down to his knees. He then pushed his foot into the man's back and his spine broke with a loud crack. John exhaled a cry as Odio pushed him to the ground. Vincent tried to catch his dad but Odio charged at him and threw him into the motorhome. He punched him in the face three times. Vincent blocked the fourth, grabbed the back of Odio's head and slammed an elbow into his face. Odio stumbled as he shook his head. Vincent kicked him in the chest but he easily caught his balance. Odio then lunged forwards and uppercut Vincent in the jaw. As Vincent fell back to the ground and felt something under his hand. Odio grabbed him and dragged him back to his feet. Vincent swung the katana at Odio and slashed his face. He grabbed for the sword and they wrestled over it for a moment. They exchanged punches and head butts until Odio tore the sword from Vincent's grip. He tried to jump aside but Odio charged him and knocked him to the ground. Odio then swung the blade down but Vincent rolled aside. A well placed kick from his position on the ground sent Odio sprawling back and caused him to drop the sword. Vincent caught it as it fell. Odio landed on the tarmac then rolled back into a kneeling position with one foot and one knee in an attempt to look composed. He looked up but couldn't see the young vampire. A hand reached under his chin and pulled his head back. He felt the tip of the cold blade against his throat.

"Wait Vincent, my friend. You…you don't need to do this," said Odio.

"It's too late, Odio. I'm sorry but I have to stop you. You already know too much," said Vincent.
With that he pushed the blade up into Odio's head and the tip pierced the top of his skull. He then pulled it out and stabbed it through the old vampire's heart. Odio's skin charred, turned to ash and he fell apart. Vincent held the burning skull in his hand until it crumbled to dust.

A weak cough came from beside the motorhome. Vincent turned and saw John trying to raise his arm.

"Vincent," wheezed John.
Vincent ran over, knelt by his side, and held his hand.

"Don't try to move dad. I'm gonna get you to a hospital," said Vincent.

"No, Vincent. Where is Alex? You have to look after him now," said John.

"Don't talk like that. It's ok. You're gonna be ok," said Vincent.

"No I'm not. I'm done," said John.

"Dad just hold on. I'll get Alex and we'll get to a hospital. Please just hold on," he said as tears welled up in his eyes.

"Vincent listen to me. Find Alex, You have to look after him now. Take him back to the airfield we arrived at when we first came to France. They will contact Andra. You have to get out of France," said John. His voice rattled wearily in his throat.

"Ok dad, I'll get Alex then we'll come and help you. We're all leaving France together," said Vincent.

"You have to contact Andra. You were right, something is wrong," John spluttered and gasped for breath.

"Dad, I'm sorry I left. I'm so sorry," Vincent said tears rolled down his face

"It's ok, son. I'm glad you came back. I couldn't save Alex, but you can. Your Mum would be proud of you. So proud. I love you son," wheeze John.

"I love you too, Dad," said Vincent.

"Go, get Alex out..." John's body went limp, his eyes rolled back in his head and he let out his final breath.

"Dad, oh dad," said Vincent.

He sat and wept while he cradled his father's body and those final words rang in his ears. He stood up and jumped up onto the motorhome. As he approached the door he heard the sounds of someone choking coming from inside. He took a few steps closer when Scarlett climbed up from the door hole. She held Alex up by his throat with one hand.

"Who are these people to you, Vincent?" she said. Her voice was raw and tears ran down her face.

"Please Scarlett. Let me explain," said Vincent.

"You better have an incredible explanation. I have just watched you help a human kill our family. You would kill vampires to save humans?" she said.

"Scarlett, please, put the boy down," he said.

"Put him down?! I should break his fucking neck!" she said.

"No! Please Scarlett, put him down and I will tell you everything," he said with his hands outstretched to her.

"Tell me everything, what do you mean?" she said.

"Please put him down," he said.

"Why should I put him down?" she said.

"Because if you don't I'll be forced to hurt you too, and believe me, Scarlett, believe me, I don't want to do that," he said.

She looked at him then to the boy and then back to Vincent. She opened her hand and dropped the boy who scampered over to Vincent. He looked at Alex and checked him for bites or cuts. Despite the tracks of his tears and some muck on his face, he was fine.

"Are you ok?" said Vincent.

"Yes, I'm ok," said Alex.

He push Alex behind him and looked back over to Scarlett.

"Ok, so explain. Who is the boy? Who is the man whose body you cried over? Vincent, why the fuck have you killed our family?" her voice broke with this last sentence.

"Because that man and this boy are my family," he said.

"W…w…What do you mean?" she said.

"I've lied to you Scarlett. The family I told you about

when we first met were a lie. That man is my father and the boy is my brother. I couldn't just let Odio and the others kill my family," he said.

"How is that man your father? He was barely in his mid-thirties. You said you were seventeen when you were bitten." Something dawned on her and Vincent saw it in her eyes. "Vincent, why were our family attacking your family?"

"Alex is the child spoken of in the prophecy. Our mother was bitten by Lord Ruhsarr while she was pregnant," he said.

"But the prophecy says that the brothers will be twins. You are a man, this boy is about ten years old," she said.

"He's eight and a half. We, are eight and a half years old. I meant to tell you on so many occasions but things were going so great I never found the right time," he said.

"Vincent… How could you lie to me like this? You could have told me. You should have told me," she said.

"I'm so sorry, Scarlett. I wish that were true but how could I have told you about this? I thought it would all be ok. I hoped the truth would never come out. The others would have tortured me to death to find Alex if they had known this," he said.

"What am I going to do? I can't just let you go, Vincent. He must be taken to Lord Ruhsarr," she said.

"That is the reason I never told you all. I can't let you do that, Scarlett. He's my brother and I am his protector. He's all that is left of my family," he said.

"He's also the destroyer of our entire fucking vampire species, Vincent!" she said.

"It will be ok," he said.

"How the fuck will it be ok?!" she said.

"Scarlett, please, calm down. We can all run away together. We'll go back to England and hide. Please come with me," he said and stepped towards her.

He grabbed her and pulled her to him. She struggled at first but then hugged him.

"I love you, Vincent," she said.

"I love you too," he said.

"If I go with you I will be betraying our species," she said.

"No. It will be ok. We've got contacts who will hide us and protect us," he said.

"I love you, Vincent, I really do, but I can't betray my species. I just can't do it," she said.

She ran her hand down his arm and her fingers landed in the handle of the Katana. She pulled it from his hand and pushed him away.

"What are you doing?" he said.

"I love you but I can't betray my people. If I cannot be with you I'd rather not be," she said.

Before Vincent could stop her she raised the blade and pushed it into her chest and through her heart.

"No!" screamed Vincent.

He pull the blade from her chest and pressed his hand to the wound but the damage was already done. Her knees gave way but he caught her and held her close.

"Why Scarlett?" he said as tears welled in his eyes.

She reached up and held his face in her hands.

"I saw you kill my family. I can't watch you kill my species. I love…"

Her sentence was cut short as her body charred. She turned to ash then fell apart in his arms. Vincent shook and let out a wail like an injured animal. The tears fell from his eyes and wet the ash that lay in his palms. He clenched them into fists and sobbed.

Alex wrapped his arms around his brother's shoulders and felt the sobs as they shook through his whole body.

"Vincent…Vincent? We need to get out of here," he said.

He turned to look at this boy, his brother. The only family, of any kind it seemed, each of them had left in the whole world. He wiped away his tears and nodded.

Vincent strained for five minutes to lift the motorhome. It was incredibly heavy but eventually, it fell back onto its wheels and the suspension creaked as it rocked back and forth. The two of them collected all the documents, passports and weapons then put them into a large hold all. They both wept as Vincent wrapped John's body in a sheet and put him in one of the bedrooms at the back of the motorhome. Vincent also wrapped Owens' body in a blanket and forcefully stuffed it in the luggage area. He smashed open all the petrol tanks of the bikes and set the whole lot on fire.

"Someone will notice this. We have to go," Alex said.

"Yes they will," said Vincent.

He half-expected one of the vampire gang to run out on fire like some 80's movie villain but they were all gone. His heart hurt with loss and betrayal but he knew he would have to focus. There would be time for mourning later. He turned the motorhome around and drove back in the direction they had come from.

"Where are we going?" said Alex.

"Back home… I mean back to the hideout," said Vincent.

"Why?" said Alex.

"Because one vampire wasn't there tonight. Destin, she must still be back at the house. I need to and get her too," said Vincent.

"Ok," said Alex

Chapter 20.

They pulled up outside the house and stepped out of the motorhome. They made their way around the back and went inside. They searched every room on the upper floors but there was no sign of Destin. Vincent then opened the basement door.

"Do we have to go down there?" said Alex.
He didn't like the thought of having to go under the house.

"Yes. We have to find her. She knows too much about us," he said then grabbed the boy and pulled him inside.

The basement was cold and the air was heavy with the smell of old blood. Vincent was used to the smell and it didn't faze him. Alex however did his best to keep the bile from rising into the back of his throat.

"Sorry, mate. Go and wait at the basement door. If anyone comes shout and I'll be there," said Vincent.

"What? No, I want to stay with you," said Alex.

"Just do as I say," said Vincent.

"Uh, ok," said Alex and trudged away.

Vincent searched the basement but Destin was gone. Everywhere he looked there were clothes and other items that reminded him of Scarlett. Every instinct screamed at him to leave but there was something he had to do. He walked to the back of the basement and down the corridor to the room where he and the vampires had stored live humans. Four people lay side by side and wrapped in layers of duct tape. Vincent took hold of a woman from the end of the row and lifted her so she could sit up. She started to scream into the gag.

"Shh, shh. Please, I'm here to help you," he said.
She continued to scream and the others began to scream
and writhe too. He placed his hands on her shoulders.

"Please be quiet. I really am here to help you," he said
in French.
The woman stopped screaming and he carefully peeled
the tape away from her mouth.

"Ok, I'm going to untie you. Don't run I need your
help," he said.

"Thank god for you, Thank god for you," she said as
she cried.
He then peeled the tape from her clothes and helped her
remove the blindfold. She wiped the tears from her green
eyes.

"What is your name?" he said.

"Louisa," she said.

"Ok, Louisa. I need you to untie these people and then
call the police," he said as he pressed a mobile phone
into her hands.

"Ok monsieur. I will help them. Thank you so much,
you have saved our lives," she said.
Vincent went to the basement door where Alex had done
as he asked and waited.

"Come on, lad. We have one more thing to do and then
we're going back to find Andra," he said.
They walked to the motorhome and Vincent went to
open the Luggage compartment.

"Shall I wait inside?" said Alex.

"Yes, I won't be long," said Vincent.
As Alex let himself into the vehicle Vincent pulled the
blood soaked body of Owens from the luggage space
and lifted it onto his shoulder. He carried it into the

woodland behind the house and soon found the mine shaft into which the vampire had been dumping the bodies of their victims. He held out the body of Owens over the shaft for a moment.

"Maybe I should say a few words before I let you go," he said, then scrunched his face into a frown. "Nah, fuck it."

He released his grip and the body fell into the darkness. It was lost to rot as just another nameless corpse.

He returned to the motorhome and started the engine. Despite the four years that had passed and all the things that happened in that time, Vincent found it surprisingly easy to figure out where they were. It took three hours to reach the airfield by which time it was around two in the morning. The Moon was high in the sky as they drove up to the gate. It looked very quiet, almost like it was abandoned. A soldier stepped out from the cabin and shouted at them in French with an English accent.

"Please calm down, sir," said Vincent.

"Stop where you are or I will shoot! Do not doubt me!" said the soldier.

Vincent put both hands out of the window. He held one up and handed the soldier their passports with the other.

"I'm Vincent Brooks, this is my brother, Alex brooks. We are all that remains of Project Nomad," said Vincent in English.

The soldier looked surprised upon hearing this man speak in a Mancunian accent. He took the passports and opened them to the photographs. He then looked from them to the brothers and back to the photos. He walked over to the cabin, picked up the phone and rang his superior.

"Hello, Sir. We have a situation at the gate. There is a man and a boy at the gate in a motorhome claiming to be Vincent and Alex Brooks. Part of the Project Nomad... No, just the two of them sir... Ok, Sir," he pressed a button in the cabin and the gates slid open.

"Head down to the command building. Left and to the end," said the soldier.

They drove through the gate and along to the Command building. As they reached it a man stepped out of the building and walked towards them. He was a short squat figure with a barrel chest which he held out with pride. He waved to them down as they approached. Two soldiers stood on either side of him with weapons ready.

"Step out of your vehicle, please," said the man. Vincent opened the driver side door and stepped down onto the tarmac. Alex followed suit and the man approached them.

"I am Captain Pinon. Private Adams, the guard on the gate, says you claim to be Project Nomad," he said in a French accent with an American twang.

"That's right. We're all that is left of Project Nomad," said Vincent.

"Do you think I am stupid? Project Nomad went dark over four years ago. You have just heard the name somewhere and thought you would play a prank at the local military airbase!"

"What do you mean 'went dark'?" said Vincent.

"There has been no contact with Project Nomad for four years," said Pinon.

"We didn't go dark, you went dark! You were supposed to help us. We haven't heard from you in all that time; not once. The shit really hit the fan tonight.

That piece of shit, Major Anthony Owens, sabotaged this motorhome and gave away our location to a group of vampires. Our father, John Brooks and Owens were killed, and you tell us we went dark?! Do me a favour, mate, get your arse back in that building. Contact Lieutenant Colonel Andra Hudson of the S.O.V.E.U. Tell her Vincent and Alex Brooks need an emergency evacuation. Tell her this safe zone has been compromised!" said Vincent.

He thrust their passports into the Captain's hands.

Pinon realised that Vincent knew too much to be lying.

"Stand down, men. Go back to your positions," he said to the soldiers.

He then scurried off back into the building. He picked up a phone and made the call.

"That was so cool," said Alex as a proud smile beamed from his face.

Vincent smiled back at him as the whole base began to wake up. Vincent and Alex were escorted inside and given food and drink and a place to rest. Alex slept on a comfy sofa but Vincent couldn't relax so he helped to put John's body into a refrigerated storage coffin for the flight back to England. Now he had time to grieve. His hands shook in both anger and sadness as he touched his dad's face for the last time. Twenty minutes later Captain Pinon approached him.

"The plane will be ready in about an hour," he said.

"Thank you, Captain. How long will the flight take?" said Vincent.

"About an hour and twenty minutes. You'll be landing in a small airbase just outside Oxford and there will be a car waiting to take you to Andra at an undisclosed location,"

"What happened to Manchester, erm, Base 115?" said Vincent.

"It was decommissioned. That is all Andra would tell me," said Pinon.

"Ok, Thank you for all your help, Captain Pinon," said Vincent.

"You are welcome," he said.

"Sorry for chewing you out before. It's been a horrible day," said Vincent.

"I accept your apology. I hope you have a pleasant flight," said Pinon.
He patted Vincent on his arm and gave him a sympathetic smile.

The hour eventually passed and they boarded the lightweight twin-engine plane. They took their seats and five minutes later the plane took off. Alex tried to sleep but Vincent sat awake as the events of the night spun like a tornado in his mind. After half an hour Alex stirred and began to cry. Vincent picked him up and lifted his brother onto his lap.

"I want dad," said Alex as the tears rolled down his face and the reality of the situation dawned on him.

"I know. It's going to be ok," Vincent said.

"How is it going to be ok? We're alone," said Alex.

"That's not true, mate, we've got friends. Remember Andra. We're going to see her soon. She'll look after us," said Vincent.

"I can only just remember her and that she is a big purple lady. I don't know her though," said Alex.

"It's ok mate. She knows you. She will keep you safe,"

said Vincent.

"She sent us to France to keep us safe. Now Dad is dead and so is Mister Owens," said Alex.

"Yes, but remember she taught Dad all sorts of fighting styles. If she hadn't taught him that you wouldn't be here now. It's obvious things got worse after we left. If we had stayed in England things would have been worse for us," said Vincent.

"I suppose," said Alex.

"It'll all be ok when we land. Andra will keep us safe, you'll see, mate. Try to get back to sleep," said Vincent. Alex rested his head on Vincent's chest and after a few minutes he was asleep. Vincent closed his eyes too and fell asleep from sheer exhaustion. Fifty minutes later the plane landed on the runway for the small airbase. The plane came to a halt and engines slowed. Vincent picked Alex up and carried him down the stairs and off the plane.

The tall slender figure of Andra stood next to a black Mercedes Benz van. She was dressed in a long coat with the hood up over her head. She looked at Vincent and her reptilian eyes were soft and friendly. She smiled at him and he tried to smile back but it never quite reached his eyes. He was still angry that they had just left them to their own devices. Despite his feelings towards her, he was happy to see a face he knew.

"Hello Vincent," she said. She looked into his eyes and put a kind hand on his shoulder. "You have both grown so much."

"You look, well, the same as when we left you," said Vincent.

Alex woke up and looked up at Andra. She waved at him

and smiled

"Hello Alex," she said to him.

"Hello," said Alex sheepishly.

"Come and get in the car. It's early and I feel I have a lot to explain," she said.

"We have some things to explain too," said Vincent. They carried John's coffin from the cargo hold of the plane and loaded it into the back of the van. They all then got into the front and Andra drove them away from the airbase. The roads were nearly empty as they drove through the streets of Oxfordshire. Most of the local human population were sleeping warm in their beds, not realising the world the night hid from them.

Chapter 21.

The van pulled up outside a big, old-looking warehouse with a sign that read 'Smith's Distribution.' The doors slid open and they drove inside. They were in a room just large enough to fit a lorry. Two soldiers stood on either side of the van. Andra drove straight up to the far wall. One of the soldiers approached the van as Andra wound down her window.

"Captain Hartley, we have the guests," she said.

"Very well ma'am," said Hartley.
He pressed his hand against the wall infront of the van. There was a faint beep and suddenly the wall in front of the car raised to reveal a spiral slope.

"Very James Bond," said Vincent with a smile.
As they drove beyond the wall he looked back and saw it sliding back into place. From this side he could see that it was a heavily reinforced door. They drove down the slope and descended to the floor below. It was a large car park full of saloons, vans, and all-terrain vehicles. The fluorescent lighting was harsh and shone off the cars making them all look brand new.

Andra parked the van in an empty bay and they all got out. Two soldiers walked up to Vincent and Alex and waved metal detectors around their bodies and legs and frisked them.

"Sorry about this but we have to be cautious these days. We had a lot of security issues after Project Nomad was put into action," said Andra
This time Vincent openly scowled at her.

"Welcome to Base 107. Please follow me," she said. "We have much to discuss."

"Damn right we do," said Vincent

"Damn right," said Alex parroting his brother.

They walked across the car park, through a doorway, down a flight of stairs, along a corridor, and into a room. Inside there was a long, pine table surrounded by comfortable office chairs. A man walked in and handed Andra a file. She took it from him and pulled out a chair.

"Vincent, Alex, please sit down. Do you want anything to eat or drink? Coffee, tea, a sandwich maybe?" she said in a friendly tone.

"Can I have a coke please?" said Alex.

"Certainly. Vincent, do you want...?"

"Cut the bullshit. You know I can't eat or drink anything you have," he said cutting her off midsentence. "I want answers. I want to know why you left us out there for nearly five years. I want to know why we never heard from you. I want to know why the man you say fought alongside you against vampires betrayed us. I had to kill him, Andra! I had to kill Owens with my bare hands. But most of all our father, who you taught to fight and who trusted you completely, lays dead in a coffin!" His voice broke with anger on the last sentence.

Andra placed the file down on the table. She looked at him and placed her hands on her hips. She then looked down at the floor and nodded. When she looked up her eyes were filled with tears.

"Usually I wouldn't allow anyone to talk to me like that... but I have failed you, and for that, I can only apologise. I had Owens psychologically evaluated before I put him on the mission. He'd had a few problems in his personal life but had been a career soldier since he was eighteen and was a deeply respected man. He passed the evaluation, I never thought for one moment that he would betray you. If I'd had even an ounce of doubt about him I would never have sent him with you," she said.

"Why did you never contact us or send anyone to check on us? We were alone out there!" said Vincent.

"We had no way of finding you besides traditional tracking and monitoring of the use of the ATM cards. Those cards were damn near untraceable though. They showed no data of the transactions that had taken place. No card number, no name, not even the amount withdrawn. If anyone had looked at the daily transactions they would just show up as a glitch. That was the purpose of them but we did too good a job. That coupled with the excellent job your dad and Owens did of staying off the radar made you invisible," she said.

"So what happened to you? I don't buy that in five years you never found one single trace of us," said Vincent.

"After you left for France the Manchester base was plagued with attack after attack. The vampires had found out where we were and they knew we were hiding something big. Luckily they never found out what that something was. A lot of our database and files were destroyed in those attacks. Eventually, we had to abandon that base and given the situation it would have been too dangerous for us to contact you and give away your location. We had to move constantly just like you. We had people undercover who tried to find you but you had disappeared off the map. As far as we knew the vampires didn't know where you were either. If Owens hadn't betrayed you, you would still have been safe.

May I ask how he betrayed you?" she said.

"My dad, Owens, and I had an argument and I left. I took up with a group of vampires but I was careful and they never learned who I really was," Vincent said. Andra raised an eyebrow at him and folded her arms across her chest.

"I know what you're thinking. How can I say you abandon us when I was literally in bed with the enemy? It was hard for me to do but I just couldn't stand to be cooped up with Owens and my dad anymore. I checked in on them at least once a week from a distance but it wasn't enough. I should have been there," he said and tears welled in his eyes. "I'm just as much to blame, I know. I was out with Scarlett, my...my...my girlfriend," said Vincent, the tears escaped his eyes and rolled down his cheeks. He took a moment to compose himself, took a deep breath, and continued. "We got back to the house we lived in and saw that all the others were riding away. We followed them and I saw that they were chasing our motorhome. I had to make a decision right there and then. My friends or my family. They attacked the motorhome and knocked it onto its side. My dad tried to defend Alex but the vampires had the advantage. That's when I chose my family. I killed my friends. I tore them apart with my bare hands and then I saw him. Owens was with the vampires. He told me he did it because he wanted to be a vampire. He tried to shoot my dad, so I crushed his skull between my hands. Oh fuck, all those vampires are dead. Scarlett killed herself, I asked her to come with us but she said couldn't live with me knowing what I had done."

Andra grabbed him and hugged him tight and he cried

into her shoulder. Great huge sobs as the emotions of the night finally flowed from him.

"Owens, that son of bitch. What a fucking arsehole. You made the right decision, Vincent. Believe me, you are achieving the role for which you were born and I'm proud of you for fucking up Owens' plan. To be honest I did expect you to leave at some point. I happen to understand what it is like to be a non-human in a human world. That is why I trained your dad and sent Owens with you. I never expected that the vampires would hit us so hard. If I had I would have done things differently but we were in a tense situation. I thought it was the right thing to do at the time. If you had stayed here you would have died or been captured. The reality of the situation is that had they found Alex they would have killed him when they found out who he was. They know he exists, they know the prophecy and they want him dead. They won't keep him in a cell, or beat him, or even try to turn him. They don't know how he will bring about the end of the vampires they just know that he will. So, they will kill him to rid the world of his threat. So you see, I too had to make a decision and maybe it was the wrong one but maybe it was the right one. I am sorry for how things panned out, I really am. I'm so sorry about your dad and Scarlett. I'm sorry about Owens too, I hope you can forgive me for that," she said.

"I'm sorry too. I know now it wasn't your fault. I understand that now, I just assumed you had forgotten about us. I'm just so angry at everything right now. I forgive you though," said Vincent as he stepped back from the hug but Andra kept one arm on his shoulder.

"I have waited for the both of you for more years than

you can imagine. Letting you go was one of the hardest decisions I've ever had to make. Your Dad raised you well, he was a good man. His fighting skills were amazing. He had the true makings of a warrior and he had a good heart. I see him in you," she said with a smile.

"I wish you could have seen him in his last stand. You taught him well. They truly outnumbered us but he never gave up, not once," said Vincent.

"He loved you both very much. You are all he had left of a family. He gave his life for you," she said.

"Now we are all that is left of our family," said Vincent.

"I know and I'm so sorry. You can stay here as long as you like, as long as you need. I know we're not biologically related but I like to think that we here are a sort of found family. I would like to think that you are part of that family too," she said.

"I would like that," said Vincent.

"Me too," said Alex.

"We need your help, now more than ever," said Vincent.

She looked at him and saw the desperate young man that in reality he was.

A man came in then with a coffee for Andra and the cola for Alex. They all sat down in the comfortable chairs.

"What made you feel so angry that you had to leave your family anyway?" said Andra as she sipped her coffee.

"I saw the letter that you wrote to my dad about me not needing to be looked after. I was jealous of Alex. I started sneaking out at night to run and that is when I met Scarlett. I fell in love with her. She was incredible. I realised that I needed to get out and I'm not too vain to admit that I acted out, thinking that I was being the big man," he said.

"I'm sorry Vincent. I didn't mean you didn't need to be looked after. I meant you were better equipped to look after yourself. I know you're only eight and a half but Alex is just a human boy while you're a fully grown vampire," she said as she looked into his eyes. "Your mum and dad would be proud of you. I know I am. You made an incredibly important and selfless decision when you put your brother's safety before your own happiness and wellbeing."

"Dad used to tell us that mum would be proud of us," said Alex.

"She would. You fought off a gang of vampires and made your way back to England unaided. Now you're here and safe. You survived the odds," she said.

"One of the vampires wasn't in the fight and got away. Destin, she possibly knows what Owens told Odio, the leader. She may think that I died along with the other vampires. She may also by now realise that I was involved. If she gets to any other vampires she will no doubt tell them and that information will in turn get to Ruhsarr. I have to find her. Alex will be safe here," said Vincent.

Andra and Alex both looked at him.

"No, we've only just got back here," said Alex.

"Yes, you should stay a while. They don't know where you are. You can hide out here for a while," said Andra.

"I've got to go. It's my duty. Alex isn't safe if she is

still out there," he said.

"No Vincent. If she does know you were involved and the vampires she tells were to find you they would torture you to get to Alex. They would probably kill you too and then you will be no use to anyone. Your brother needs you and you could do with some R&R yourself, and maybe some training. Also, it would be helpful to this operation to scientifically study a fully grown vampire. If you're willing to help that is. Most vampires are…reluctant, at best to help on that part," said Andra with a smile.

"Ok, ok. I'll stay…for a while," he said.

"Good, I'll have some quarters set up for you," she said with a smile.

"Yay, Vincent's staying," sang Alex.
Vincent smiled and ruffled his brother's hair.

Three weeks passed and the brothers settled in well to their new home. Alex coped with the day to day things. He had more than enough toys and video games to keep him occupied. Andra taught him maths, English and, science. At night the death of his dad still haunted his nightmares and sometimes he would wake up crying and screaming.

Vincent would guard his room while he slept and was always on hand if he needed comforting. He attempted to sleep a few times too, though it was more like meditation than actual sleep. He could take it or leave it but he felt more relaxed if he had slept. He found living among humans difficult after years of living with vampires. He had gotten used to giving in to his urges to hunt and feed on them. These urges almost overwhelmed him in the first few days but he learned techniques to manage them and keep control over his base needs. As time passed he started to despise what he was. Vampires had taken everything from him: His mum and dad, his grandparents, his lover, and most of all his humanity. He couldn't even just feed from humans like other vampires. His vampirism cursed him to be forced to take their lives or see them bound to this curse just as he was.

Andra talked to the members of the S.O.V.E.U. to set up a blood donation service. Each soldier gave a pint of blood every two months and it was enough to keep him sustained. The science department worked with him to create a synthesised blood substitute. It had all the base elements of blood but it didn't quite replicate the real thing.

Andra worked out a training schedule for Vincent and Alex. They worked out in the gym four times a week. Here they discovered that Vincent was stronger and faster than most vampires. He had suspected he might be seeing as he was the offspring of the original vampire. Alex also began to show some interesting abilities of his own.

"You are getting strong, Alex. It seems it wasn't only Vincent who went through changes when you're mother was bitten. Obviously, you're not as strong as a vampire but you are faster and stronger than a human of your own age," said Andra.

"Alex the superboy," said Vincent with a smile. Alex flexed his arms and put his balled up fist on his hips like superman… and then laughed as Vincent tickled his neck.

Chapter 22.

Destin hiked along a path somewhere high up in the Himalayan Mountains. She was being guided by two vampires, Hosan and Ris, who had kept her blindfolded for most of the journey. She now had no idea where she was.

Ris walked closer behind her, took hold of the strip of material and pulled it away from her eyes. For the first time that day she could see. The path they walked on was only lit by a lantern carried by Hosan who walked ahead of her. They approached the mouth of a cave that had been carved into the side of the mountain. It was roughly nine feet high. As they walked in there was an opening bored into the wall to the left. The resulting corridor continued for six feet then turned to the right for six feet, then right again for six feet, and then to the left. They walked down this corridor for another twenty feet. It had been carved this way to keep out the sunlight in the daytime. The corridor opened up into the huge expansive hall akin to that of a palace. It had been hand carved into the black rock of the mountain. Destin's jaw dropped open as her eyes scanned the hall.

"This must have taken years to create," she said.

"I've been told it took six vampires two weeks for this hall. The whole excavation for all the rooms took just over six months," said Ris.

"Wow," said Destin.

"The walls, floor, and ceiling had to be carved flat and polished smooth. The construction was completed over one hundred years before I came here," he said.

Tapestries, paintings, and all manners of art adorned the walls and the entire room was lit with candles. Musicians played music on old instruments that Destin had never seen the likes of. Vampires who wore next to nothing danced on the tables. More vampires sat around feeding from humans who were tied to the tabletops. Other humans were locked in cages or bound up with chains and rope. There were bodies piled up in a corner and the air was thick with the smell of human death. Two vampires stood up from a table as they argued over a human male. This quickly escalated to them exchanging punches until a huge vampire barged in and broke it.

"Shut up, both of you," he roared.
He slammed both their heads together and threw them in opposite directions. He then grabbed the man by the throat and walked away. Other vampires sang Old Norse and Celtic songs while others chanted ancient rhymes in dead languages.

Hosan and Ris led Destin passed all this chaos and across the hall. They stopped at the doorway to a room that was completely devoid of light. Their vampire eyes could see something enormous as it moved in the darkness. There was a whimper, the scent of human blood, and the sound of someone feeding. Hosan and Ris stood on either side of Destin.

"Why do you disturb me?" hissed a deep, guttural voice.

"Master, we have brought this young woman to you," said Hosan.

"And why have you brought her to me?" said the

voice.

"She has information she says you need to hear, sir. She would not relay it to us. She said she will speak only to you," said Hosan.

"This information must be extremely valuable. Speak then, woman! Reveal this information that you feel is so important you must disturb me while I feed," said the voice.

"I…I…I know the…the location of the prophesised child," said Destin.

There was a pause then the enormous thing moved and stepped out from the darkness. Blood dripped from his jaws and the body of a naked woman twitched in his hand. Destin had been told of Ruhsarr's appearance from other vampires but had never truly believed the tales. She was overcome with awe and fell to her knees.

"My lord, my master, forgive me for disturbing you," she said.

He was completely unfazed by her display of awe and adoration. He turned, placed the woman on the floor, and brushed his huge bloody hand through her hair. She lurched up into a sitting position and screamed as the vampirism altered her flesh. Ruhsarr looked at Destin.

"Well then, come on. Out with it, reveal the location of the child," he said.

"He was in Toulouse, France, but I think he may have escaped back to England," said Destin.

"Where did you attain this information?" said Ruhsarr.

"A man named Owens. He claimed to be English and part of a group of vampire hunters. He came to our hideout four months ago. He told us that he knew the boy and that he had been protecting him. He also told us he would take us to him in exchange for being turned. My leader, Odio, and my friends went with him, none of them ever came back. I found their bikes smashed and burned but no sign of Owens. There were the remains of human blood from two humans and ash from my on the ground, sir. I could smell it," said Destin.

"This man, Owens, he mentioned a group of vampire hunters. Did he mention their name?" said Ruhsarr.

"Not that I can remember, my Lord, but he did say that he was in the military," said Destin.

"Hmm, interesting. Thank you for bringing me this information, my child. What is your name?" said Ruhsarr with a smile.

"My name is Destin, my Lord," she said.

"Well, Destin, please, make yourself at home. You are among friends here. Feed, dance, and be happy," he said.

"Thank you, my lord," she said.

"Thank you too, Destin," he said.

"If there is anything you need and I can be of service please ask me, my Lord. I am your humble servant," she said.

"Yes, Thank you, Destin," he said.
She walked backward away from him bowing and curtsying.

"Anything, my Lord," she said.

"Go and feed and have fun, now!" he said.
She turned and hurried back into the hall and looked at all the delights to be had.

Ruhsarr turned to the vampire to the right.

"Hosan, send this information to Dienco, my Chief of Military Operations. He has my soldiers searching in every country of the world. Tell him to call them all back and focus their efforts in England. I want this child found and I want him dead," he said.

"Yes, my Lord, as you command," said Hosan. He then ran off across the hall, through the cavernous rooms of the Ruhsarr lair. He finally arrived in a communications room. He sat down at a computer. He clicked on the internet logo and waited a few moments while it connected to the internet via a satellite broadcast. He wrote an email containing all the information Destin had told Ruhsarr and his orders then sent it to Dienco. Dienco then in turn relayed this information to the soldiers.

The woman Ruhsarr had just drunk from stood up for her first time as a vampire. She looked at Ruhsarr and was overtaken by an immediate compulsion to bow down to him. He put his index finger under her chin and stood her up straight.

"Hello, little one. What is your name?" he said.

"Michelle," she said.

"Well, Michelle, I am Lord Ruhsarr. I have saved you from clutches of death itself. Do you know why I saved you?" he said with a devious smile.

"No, sir," she said.

"Because I am powerful and generous. Aren't I?" he said.

"Yes you are, sir," she said.

So, Michelle. Whom do you serve?" he growled.

"You and only you, my Lord. The powerful and mighty Lord Ruhsarr," she said.

"Yes. Yes, you do," he said. His smile widened as he gnashed his serrated teeth together.

Chapter 23.

December 2003.

The two brothers celebrated their birthday together for the first time in four years. They were sat at the table in Andra's quarters and Alex was eating his evening meal at the table while Vincent read the book Andra had bought him. She disappeared into her kitchen and came out with a cake that had nine lit candles. She began to sing and the brothers smiled at each other.

"Happy birthday, little dude," said Vincent.

"Happy birthday, big dude," said Alex.

"Now, no fighting about who blows the candles out. Work together," said Andra as she placed the cake on the table.

They looked at each other and smiled.

"Thank you, Andra. This is fantastic," said Vincent.

"Don't mention it. You both deserve to be happy after the year you've had," she said.

Alex smiled and quickly blew out all the candles.

"Well, you cheeky thing," said Andra with a smile.

"Relight them with your fire breath," said Vincent.

"No, there will be no table left, never mind the cake," she said with a smile.

She pulled a Zippo lighter from her pocket and relit the candles.

"Your turn, Vincent," said Alex.

Vincent smiled at him again and blew out the candles. For the rest of the night they played games and watched films. It was the happiest they had both felt in a long time.

While they were in France John had been teaching
Alex what he could. Now he was back with Andra she
began educating him about subjects he had missed out
on. He was learning at an incredible rate but she also
wanted him to go to school to interact with children his
age. All his life had been around adults. He and his
brother were the same age but with Vincent being a
vampire and fully grown they had more of an older and
younger sibling relationship rather than that of twins.
She put plans together to send him to live two days a
week with a family. A man and woman named Roger
and Sarah Booth. They were both been soldiers in the
S.O.V.E.U. and had both seen active service in Iraq.
Roger had been in the Army and Sarah in the Air Force.
They already had two adopted children named Andrew
and Mary, and in the past year both of them had retired
from the armed forces. Having more time on their hands
they had applied to be foster parents. Andra had
approached them with the idea as it wouldn't seem
suspicious if Alex lived with them too.

Roger was tall with a stocky build and short cropped
blonde hair. Sarah was slightly shorter with a slim,
athletic build with long black hair and the bluest eyes
Alex had ever seen. Her father was English and her
mother was Peruvian. They lived in Didcot near Oxford
in a four-bedroom semi-detached house. Alex met them
for the first time just before New Year's Day and
instantly felt safe in their company. A few days later he
spent his first night with them. A week late Andra sat
him down at the kitchen table in the Booth's house.

They had a serious conversation about his first day at school, and she gave him some strict instructions.

"Do not tell anyone about your past. Not about the motorhome, vampires, or me. If anyone asks questions about your parents tell them they had died in a car accident while you were living in France. You were there because your dad found a job there. Roger and Sarah are your foster parents. Listen to them and your teachers and do as you are told. Do not get into any fights with the other children. You can't risk it. You are far stronger than they are and you will hurt them. Do you understand?" Andra said to him.

"Yes ma'am," Alex said.

"Good. Now, go and play," she said.
He jumped down from the chair and ran into the back garden of their house where Andrew and Mary were waiting for him.

"What do you hope he will gain from this experience?" said Vincent.

"I hope he will make new friends and he will be educated in subjects that I can't teach him. There are things that he can learn here that he won't learn with us on the base. He needs to have a childhood. Our line of work and lifestyle aren't an ideal environment for a growing child," said Andra.

"To be fair he isn't a normal child," said Vincent.

"That's not the point. He has to live and blend in with today's society. Being a child and acting like an adult will make him stand out too much. He can't afford to cause any suspicion about his identity," said Andra.

The next day he went to the local school and was glad to be in the same class as Andrew and Mary to help him settle in. The class teacher, Miss Barns, introduced him to the other children and he waved as they all said, "Hello, Alex."

In his first week some of the kids made fun of his Mancunian accent but he just took it as a joke and made fun of them too.

Miss Barns, found that he was keen to learn. He was very good at sports and even managed to get a trial for the football team.

A few months passed and he settled in without a hitch. Everything was going fine until he was kicked out of the football team for fighting with another boy. They argued and fought over who was going to collect the ball after training. As a result he was taken to the head teacher, Mr. Woodley.

"I will not tolerate fighting in my school. Do you understand young man?" he said.

"Yes sir," Alex said.

"Tony is going to have to be off school for the rest of the week," said Mr. Woodley.

"I know, I am sorry sir. It won't happen again," said Alex.

"Yes, I know it won't. There are consequences for our actions…" said Mr. Woodley.

At that point Alex's attention trailed off as he didn't mind getting told off by the teachers. That same night Roger and Sarah took him to see Andra. He trembled as he sat in the chair waiting for her. The teachers he could handle, but Andra was the tallest person he knew and was scary when she was angry. The fact that she was a dragon and he had been told that she could breathe fire only made her even scarier.

The door swung open, she walked into the white walled room and glared at him. Roger and Sarah both stood to attention. The tension in the room was palpable. Alex felt his stomach churn in fear. There was a look in her eye that made him want to run away and hide. She slammed the report folder down on the table.

"When I first sent you to live with Roger and Sarah what was the most important thing I told you to do?!" she said.

"Not to bring attention to myself," mumbled Alex.

"What was that? I don't speak mumble!" she said.

"Not to bring attention to myself, ma'am," he said in a clear voice.

"Not to bring attention to yourself," she repeated. "And how long have you been at the school?"

"T…Two month, m…ma'am,"

"Two months! Roger, Sarah, and I have been trying very hard to make this work. We made sure all the foster papers went through. We have made sure no one could find out where you came from. We ensured all your paperwork made you appear to be like any other foster child. Vampires have spies everywhere. Not a single word had been misspelt and every single page of the paperwork had been scrutinised. Then you go and nearly wreck it all because you got into a fight!" she said.

"Mr. Sayers had told me to collect the ball but Tony wanted to take it. Tony grabbed it and I went to take it off him. He pushed me so I pushed him back," said Alex.

"What else happened?" she said.

"Nothing ma'am," he said.

"Are you sure?" she said.

"No," he mumbled as he looked down at his feet.

"Alex, look at me… What else?" she said, her voice was ice cold.

Alex looked up. Her eyes were hard and angry.

"I… might have punched him a bit and thrown him down," said Alex.

"You might have?! You punched him three times and chipped four of his teeth. You then swung him around and threw him ten feet across the yard," said Andra.

"But ma'am, Mr. Sayers told me to bring the ball not Tony. Why do I have to follow rules? Tony doesn't," said Alex.

"Because Tony is an ordinary nine year old boy! You're too strong to fight with people your own age. I told you that but you either forgot or chose to ignore my rules. If Tony gets in trouble he will get shouted at by his Mum and Dad. If you get in trouble you will have to move again to a new town with new people." Andra turned to talk to Roger and Sarah. "I think I have contained this and hopefully there will be no repercussions from it. You all need to be vigilant for the next few days. If anything unusual happens, you feel like you're being watched or notice strange people hanging around call me straight away."

"Yes ma'am," said Roger and Sarah.

She turned her attention back to Alex.

"I gave you those rules for a good reason and I trusted you. Can I trust you to follow them from now on?" she said.

He looked at the floor and a tear rolled down his cheek as he nodded.

"Yes ma'am. I'm really sorry, ma'am. I won't let it

happen again. I honestly didn't mean to hurt Tony. I'm so sorry ma'am," he said

Andra scooped him up out of the chair and hugged him. Her words were softer now but there was still a seriousness in her voice.

"I know you are, make sure this never happens again. You will have plenty of time for fighting when you grow up. I don't want to be angry at you, I'm trying to look after you. You can't fight with your classmates. Is that understood? It will only lead to bad things as one mistake could affect us all. Promise me that you won't get into trouble again," she said.

"I won't, ma'am, I promise. I won't get in any more trouble," he said.

"Ok, Vincent is in the other room. Go and see him. I need to talk with Roger and Sarah," said Andra.

Alex walked into the next room and closed the door. He was now in a cafeteria with a kitchenette along one wall, a coffee machine, and a table and chairs in the middle. Vincent was sat at the table, holding a cup of coffee while he listened to his mp3 player. He looked at Alex and smiled.

"Can you drink that?" said Alex.

"No. I just love the smell of it. You should stay out of trouble, little dude," said Vincent.

"I know, I'm sorry," said Alex.

"You don't have to apologise to me. You shouldn't fight with other kids, you're too strong and it will keep you from getting in trouble with Andra," said Vincent.

"She's scary when she's angry," said Alex.

"I know, she went easy on you today too. Imagine what she is like with the soldiers," said Vincent.

"I don't really want to," said Alex.

"Don't worry. Here eat this. I made it just before Andra told you to come in here," said Vincent and pushed a plate with jam on toast towards Alex. He then put his headphones on his brother's ears.

"What this?" said Alex.

"It's a playlist of metal songs I like. There is stuff from the 70s, 80s and 90s in there. You like it?" said Vincent.

"Yeah, it's awesome," said Alex and smiled. He bit into a slice of toast and then nodded his head to the music in the way he had seen done by Vincent. Vincent smiled and ruffled his brother's hair.

Chapter 24.

May 2004.

The next six months passed without incident and life was good for Alex. For the first time in his life he had a sense of stability. His nights were still haunted by nightmares of the night his Dad died but his health and wellbeing were improving. He was getting used to the two nights a week that he spent with the Booth family and finally had a sense of belonging. He liked Roger and Sarah, he liked Andrew and Mary too. He liked that they had dinner at the table together. On the weekends they went out as a family and they went on holidays. Alex was quickly incorporated into their family and made to feel like one of their own. He learned to play as a child too. The kind of games kids play at his age. They would argue too the way that kids do. Roger and Sarah always made sure they apologised to each other and made up. It was all done to instill a sense of responsibility in Andrew and Mary but especially in Alex.

Sometimes Vincent and Andra would have meetings with Roger and Sarah. Andra would only come in when Andrew and Mary were in bed. She thought it would take too much to explain who and what she was to them. Also, the less they knew made them less of a possible target.

When Alex and Vincent were sat at the kitchen table talking while Andra, Roger and Sarah went over plans in another room. The brothers still spoke to each other in a way more akin to that of older and younger siblings.

"Hey, did I tell you Andra has given me a job?" said

Vincent.

"No, that's great. What do you do?" said Alex with a smile on his face.

"I spy on vampires," said Vincent.

"Like that Bond guy? He's a spy. Do you drive cool cars and fight bad guys," said Alex.

"Not quite, little dude. I watch vampire safe houses and infiltrate their nightclubs. I'm the perfect man for the job. I have the advantage of being a vampire so I blend right in," said Vincent.

"What will you do when you get in, beat them all up?" said Alex.

"No. Hopefully, it won't come to that. I get to know them and let them think that we're friends. When they think they can trust me they will tell me their secrets. The trick is to never get too close to anyone so they don't see through my story," said Vincent.

"What do you mean, secrets? Like where they keep their weapons?" said Alex.

"Sometimes, but mostly where people will be at certain times," said Vincent

"Ugh, that's boring," said Alex and rolled his eyes.

"It's a lot more interesting than it sounds," said Vincent as he laughed.

"How do you stop yourself from getting too close to people?" said Alex.

"You keep your private life to yourself and don't get involved with anyone on any level beyond being just friends. I learnt that lesson the hard way," Vincent said with a grave look on his face.

"You still miss Scarlett, don't you," said Alex.

"Yes, some days more than others. We had some great

times together you know. I wish things had turned out different but we can't change the past. That's beside the point though right now. The point is I might have to go undercover, so I might not be able to come around and see you as much as we both would like. I'll still keep an eye on you. So, even though I might not be able to visit you like this I will be still look out for you. Ok?" said Vincent.

"Yes, ok. I understand," said Alex.

"Come here and give me a hug," said Vincent. Alex jumped down from his chair and hugged his brother.

Andra and Vincent said goodnight to Roger, Sarah and Alex. They got in Andra's car and drove back to the base. Later that night they were talking about a nightclub that had opened up in London.

"It's called The Bone Shack. It's located here in Charing Cross," she said pointing to it on a map. "I want you to go in, take a look around and become familiar with the bar staff and management. My leads have presented me with documents that confirm a firstborn vampire named Gilda owns the club; possibly the building too."

"What do I do once I'm in there?" he said.

"I want you to find out if and when Gilad will be there. If you get a chance to meet her be careful. My spies say she has an extremely powerful glamour ability. Don't let her get into your head. The main objective is to find out if she knows the location of the other members of The Children of the Blood," she said.

"The Children of the Blood?" he said.

"Yes, did Odio not tell you about them?" she said.

"No," he said.

"That's weird. I just assumed that was information that all vampires passed along to each other," said Andra.

"Nope. Not to me anyway," said Vincent.

"Ok well, here goes. They are the first vampires Ruhsarr made when he gained his vampirism. He fed them the blood of the dragon, Azangor. The same blood that made him as strong and fucked up as he is. It made them even more powerful than they already were. Hence the name Children of the Blood. The first of them being Dienco, he is the head of the vampire military operation. Then Gilad, she is the head of their business operations though she acts like some sort of mafia boss. Saltorg is their head of technological research, both for medical and real-world applications. Jorshean was their physical abilities researcher, though she disappeared about four hundred years ago and has not seen since. Their offspring make up the five main clans: Ruhsarrian, Diencosa, Gilady, Saltrogion, and Jorsheantah," she said.

"Does that make Alex and me members of our own clan due to our mum being bitten by Ruhsarr?" he said. Andra looked at him and raised one eyebrow then smiled.

"Yes, I suppose it does. As a result you must be careful. You won't smell like these vampires so they might be able to detect you through scent. Even after all these years we still don't know everything about them so keep your eyes peeled and your wits about you," she said.

"Yes ma'am. When do I go?" he said.

"Tomorrow, we still have some things to prepare," she said.

The next day was uneventful, mostly consisting of the two of them going over the plans for the next few weeks. They talked over a few final things as they walked through the base to the garage.

"OK, repeat your back story to me," said Andra.

"My name is Jake Walker. I was born and grew up in Leeds until I was turned at the age of twenty five and have lived in London for six years," he said.

"Where do you live in London?" she said.

"On Helena road, near Gladstone Park," he said.

"How long since you were turned?" she said.

"I was turned in 1994 by a girl I met in a nightclub," he said.

"Ok, are you ready?" she said

"Yes ma'am," he said.

They were now standing next to a car made to look like a taxi with a driver sitting inside.

"Your driver is Tommy, he'll drive you over to the club. Go in, mingle and snoop around but don't draw too much attention to yourself. Keep in contact, if anyone starts sniffing around or gets too close, make your excuses and get out," she said.

"Yes ma'am," he said.

She slapped her hand on his shoulder and then hugged him, "Now go. Remember, look after yourself. You have a mission but you don't want to look like you have a stick up your arse, so, try to have some fun too," she said.

"Is that an order?" he said.

"Damn right it is," she said with a smile.

He smiled at her and got in the car.

Chapter 25.

Vincent visited the Bone Shack for four nights in a row and got to know the layout of the club. The first floor was set out as a metal club with most of the walls painted black except for the bar which was painted blood red. There were band posters and flyers pinned to the walls around some of the seating areas and the corridor which lead to the toilets. Signed photos of band members adorned the walls around the pool table and a Jägermeister flag was pinned to the ceiling above it. The dance floor was varnished with dark wood stain and the DJ stood in a booth designed to look like the pulpit of a church with an upturned cross on the front. The upper floor was exclusively for VIPs.

"You can go to the upper floor if you like," said the purple haired bartender as Vincent approached her on the fourth night.

"Sorry, are you talking to me?" he said.

"Yes. I know one of our kind when I see us. You have access to the VIP floor privileges," she said.

"Oh, I…" he said.

"Don't worry. You don't have to hide in here. Just show your teeth to Hans at the barrier," she said then gave him a little smile that just about showed off her own fangs.

"Ok, thanks for the tip," he said.

"No problem," she said and gave him a wink.

He walked to the stairs and a huge stoic vampire looked him up and down. Vincent showed him his fangs and Hans unclipped the rope barrier from across the stairs.

"Have a nice night, sir," said Hans with a smile.

"Thank you," said Vincent.

As he reached the top of the stairs he looked around. There was a large area with vampires sitting around tables and talking. There were booths off to the sides, some with the curtains pulled across and some without. A tall man with long dreadlocks stood up and walked over to him.

"Hello. I'm the manager, my name is Bose. You're welcome to try one of our many blood givers. We have tastes to satisfy all palettes," he said in a London Accent as he handed Vincent an ornate leather menu. Vincent opened it and saw it contained people's names with their blood types written under each one.

"Thank you Bose but I'm ok for now," said Vincent.

"Very well. Please, feel free to relax and enjoy the atmosphere and good company," said Bose. Vincent then followed Bose back to the table and sat down. He introduced himself and began talking to the vampires who he learned came from all walks of life. Slowly he turned the conversation to the ownership of the club.

"Have you met Gilad?" someone asked.

"Obviously, I've heard of her but I can't say I've ever had the privilege of meeting her," said Vincent.

"She will be in this Wednesday. I'll introduce you to her. I have a feeling that she will like you very much. You're defiantly her type," said Bose.

"That would be fantastic. Thank you, Bose," said Vincent.

Two nights later Vincent walked into the VIP area and

was greeted by Bose and two large, serious looking men dressed in black suits.

"Hi, Jake. These two men are Gilad's bodyguards. She is here and I have told her that you would like to meet her. She has agreed but you have to be searched for any weapons first." Said Bose.

"Ok," said Vincent with a nod.

"Please raise your arms," said one of the bodyguards. He did as they asked and they frisked him. When they were happy they let Bose escort him to Gilad's own personal booth. They approached the table where a tall woman with long, black hair that glimmered in the lights and wore a red, strapless dress was sat talking to a few of the regular customers.

"Lady Gilad," said Bose.

"Yes," said Gilad.

"Please allow me to introduce Jake Walker. He has expressed an interest in meeting you in person. Jake this is Lady Gilad," said Bose.

"Well, hello Jake Walker," she said as she looked him up and down.

"Hello, Lady Gilad. It's an honour to meet you," said Vincent.

"And you, Jake. Please, have a seat," she said.

"Thank you," said Vincent as he sat down.

"Tell me something. Why should I care that you want to meet me?" said Gilad.

"I wanted to meet you because I've heard so much about you from a gang I used to run with. Eventually, we parted ways, so when I came to London and was told that you own this club I knew I had to meet you," said Vincent.

"Really? So what did they used to say about me?" said Gilad.

"They used to argue about who was the most powerful vampire and your name was mentioned every time. They also said you were beautiful but may I say, their words do your beauty no justice," said Vincent.

"That's very kind of you to say, Jake. I must warn you, there are three things I love most in this world. Blood, beautiful men, and flattery," said Gilad as she raised an eyebrow and smiled.

"Thank you, m'lady," said Vincent.

"Please, call me Gilad," she said.

They spoke long into the early hours and she even asked him some questions about himself. All the preparation he and Andra had done pulled him out of some tight situations. Despite all his efforts to get her to talk about the other members of the Children of the Blood she didn't reveal anything useful.

Vincent looked at his watch and realised there was a little over an hour until sunrise.

"This has been amazing but I'm going to have to go," he said as he stood up.

"You can stay here for the day if you like," she said.

"That's very kind of you but I really must go," he said.

"I hate to see you leave but if you have to go I can't stop you," she said.

"Thank you for a great night. I hope to see you again sometime soon," he said.

Gilad stood up and wrapped her arms around him and kissed him on the lips.

"Yes, I hope to see you soon," she said.

She let him go and he walked away from the booth.

When he walked down the stairs she leaned towards her bodyguards.

"He doesn't taste like any other vampire I've ever met. Don't let him leave," she whispered.

Vincent reached the bottom of the stairs and noticed some of the bouncers looking over at him. He looked back up the stairs and saw the bodyguards following him. There was only a handful of people left in the club so he swiftly walked towards the exit but the doormen blocked his path. One of the bouncers grabbed Vincent by the shoulder but was quickly thrown onto the floor. Vincent then twisted the man's arm until the bones snapped. Another bouncer threw a punch at the back of Vincent's head but he ducked under their arm. He grabbed the bouncer's leg and pulled it from under him. As the man fell Vincent moved swiftly, grabbed his head, and slammed it into the floor so hard his skull collapsed. He then walked towards the doormen but was grabbed and thrown to the floor by one of the bodyguards. He got to his feet but the second bodyguard ran into him and they both crashed into the wall beside the doors. Vincent punched the guard in the face three times then spun him around and threw him across the room. As he was about the step towards the exit again all his muscles tensed and a burning sensation ran over the entire surface of his body. He turned his head as much as possible and saw the first bodyguard holding a taser gun. The second bodyguard ran over and punched him. Their fist connected with Vincent's jaw so hard that, for the first time in his life, Vincent lost consciousness.

Chapter 26.

Andra and Vincent had an arrangement that he would contact her at least once a day. This would be at the most a visit to the base and at the least a text message that simply read "V". So after two days passed and he hadn't been in contact she became concerned. When a week passed and he hadn't been back to the base she began to worry. She walked from her quarters to the science department and approached Sergeant Major Fletcher. A tall, slim man with blonde hair that was greying hair at his temples. He was the head science officer on the base and had worked within the S.O.V.E.U. for a few years.

"Hi Fletcher," she said.

"Hello, Ma'am," he said.

"I've been told Vincent Austin spends some of his free time in here, is that correct?" she said.

"Yes. He usually comes in here at night as he doesn't sleep much. I've got to know him over the past few months. He's an intelligent guy. Is there something wrong?" he said.

"Possibly. He's been working in the field for the past two weeks. He was in contact for the first week but then he just fell off the radar. I'm just concerned and wondering if you've seen him?" she said.

"No ma'am. I can't say I have," he said.

"Do you know he's a vampire?" she said.

"Yes. I have seen enough vampires to know one when I see one. He's here with your consent though so if you trust him that's good enough for me," he said.

"He went off with a gang of vampires in the past but this is different. I just don't think that he would disappear like this. Not after all that has happened to him in the past year," she said.

"Not to sound like I'm questioning your judgement ma'am but how do you know?" he said.

"He's told me on many occasions that he no longer has any interest in others of his own kind. He hates being a vampire and has realised that he is his brother's protector. They are very close now since the death of their dad. Just disappearing out of the blue would go against all that he holds dear now," she said.

"What about his relationship with other people here? Does anyone else have a problem with him?" he said.

"None that I know of. He's even friendly with me these days," she said.

"I can trace his phone signal, which could lead us right to him or at least triangulate his last know location," he said.

"That sounds good. How about also looking into the CCTV feed for London?" she said.

"We can try that. The firewall for that network has become a little more difficult to get around since the last time we did that but it's nothing we can't figure out," he said.

"Hmm. Ok, do what you can and let me know if you find anything," she said.

"Will do, ma'am," he said.

"Thanks, Fletcher," she said and walked away.

Chapter 27.

Vincent had come around in the back of a van surrounded by vampires. He tried to fight but they outnumbered and they quickly pinned him down. He struggled with them but was injected with something and fell unconscious.

Hours later he woke up in a dark unlit cell. It was almost pitch black but his vampire eyes could make out the walls and heavy iron door. Near that door stood a bottle, by the smell of its content he knew exactly what was inside; human blood. The smell was intoxicating and called to his instincts. It reminded him of Scarlett and all the atrocities he had committed. He had tried to suppress the memories of what he was and what he had done but that smell made them all come rushing back. His head spun, his stomach lurched and he threw up all over the concrete floor

He was woken by the sound of the door being unlocked. It then burst open and four vampires ran in. He fought with them, killing one as he punched his fist straight through their heart. The others jumped on him and held him down. More followed and he felt the sting of an injection again and his vision faded.

He woke up strapped to a cold, stainless steel table in the middle of a large round room. To him it looked like an old, white, tiled operating theatre from the 19th century except all the equipment was modern. There were rows of wooden seats going high up into the room. In every seat sat a vampire and they were all looking at him. He struggled but the straps that held his limbs were made from some kind of incredibly strong fibre.

A man who wore a rubber surgical apron and surgical mask approached him.

"Where is Andra?" said the man in an undiscernible Eastern European accent.

Vincent looked at the man but didn't reply.

"Where is Andra?!" he said in a stern tone.

Vincent still didn't reply, he just looked the man up and down and gave out a little laugh. The man stepped away from the table and returned with a hammer.

"Where is Andra?" repeated the man.

Again Vincent didn't reply. The man placed the hammer over Vincent's right hand.

"Where…is…Andra?" he said.

"Oh do fuck off," said Vincent.

The man raised the hammer and brought it down onto the palm of Vincent's hand. He screamed through gritted teeth and then looked the man dead in the eyes.

"Fuck you," he said.

The man struck Vincent's hand again several times. The hits broke two of his fingers, his thumb, and all of his metacarpal bones. Vincent tried to stifle a screams.

"Andra, Andra, I don't recall?" he said with a smile.

The man hit him again.

"Your hand looks a bit of a mess, Mr. Walker. You know, you can stop this right now. All you have to do is tell me the location of Andra Hudson."

Vincent composed himself.

"I'm not at liberty to reveal that information... I suppose you already know what I am, so just to inform you, my bones will heal before I leave this room," said Vincent.

"I know that your bones will heal. I'm not trying to disfigure you, Jake. Oh no, no. I'm trying to hurt you," said the man.

He stepped away from the table again and returned this time with a pair of bolt cutters. He placed the blades on either side of Vincent's little finger.

"Where is Andra?" he said in a jolly tone.

Vincent again refused to answer. The man squeezed the handles of the bolt cutters together and the blades snapped shut. Vincent screamed in agony as his finger rolled off the table and burned up as it hit the floor.

"Now, where is Andra?" said the man.

Vincent still refused to answer. The man moved the blades of the bolt cutters to the next finger and snapped them shut again. This went on for hours until only the thumb remained on Vincent's right hand but he still wouldn't answer the question.

"Take him back to his cell. Make him drink some blood. I want him in a cognitive state," said the man to his orderlies.

Back in his cell Vincent refused to drink the blood. The orderlies beat and tased him. He gripped one of them around the neck and squeezed. Blood began to pour from the orderlies eyes. The other orderly screamed and ten guards ran in. They held Vincent down and strapped him to a chair. They forced a tube down his throat and pumped the blood directly into his stomach. He wrenched his arm free and forced his fingers down his throat in an attempt to make himself vomit. They strapped him down with stronger restraints and after that he was strapped to the chair nearly every hour of the day and night.

The orderlies came into his cell the next day and injected him while he was still strapped to the chair. When he came round he was strapped to the table again. All his fingers had grown back since they had been so cruelly liberated from his hands just twelve hours before. No one said a word. They simply cut off all his newly regrown fingers and sent him back to his cell. They repeated this process for nine days in a row. Then, after what seemed, to Vincent, like two days the orderlies came into his cell and injected him again. Again awoke strapped to the table and again the man approached him holding the bolt cutters.

"Where is Andra?" said the man.

"Oh, not this bollocks again," said Vincent with a sigh.

"Where is Andra?" said the man.

"Kiss my hairy ball sack you fucking cunt," said Vincent, he spat his words at the man.

"Where is Andra?" he said more insistently.

"I don't know and if I did what makes you think I would tell a fuckwit like you?" said Vincent.
A look of anger fell across the man's face.

"What you gonna do? Cut more of my fingers off? Go ahead, start with these," said Vincent and raised his middle fingers. "It won't make me tell you."
The man place the bolt cutters down on the top of a stainless steel trolley that was covered with a blood soaked, white sheet.

"Not today. Today we are going to try something, different?" said the man with a smile that was filled with malice. He then looked towards a pair of the orderlies.

"Open the shutter."

The orderlies pulled a long chain that ran up one of the walls and across the ceiling. It was attached to a square panel set into the roof directly above Vincent. All the vampires stepped back to a safe distance into the shade as a beam of sunlight hit Vincent. He writhed and screamed and pulled at his restraints for a moment. He stopped when he realised nothing was happening. His torturer and all the spectator's mouths hung open as they couldn't believe what they were seeing. They then turned to each other and began to whisper. Five minutes passed by slowly and Vincent realised he had never stood in the light of the sun for this length of time. He had just always assumed that it would harm him. As he lay there he could feel its pleasant warmth caressing his skin. Soon his flesh began to tingle. Just a little at first but then the feeling became an itch. Soon it was uncontrollable and all over his body. It then became a burning sensation and the pain began to rise. He screamed in agony as his skin began to smoulder and smoke until flames shot from his flesh. The spectators screamed too as they tried to scrabble over each other in an attempt to avoid the flames.

"Shut the vent and put out the flames! He's no good to me dead!" shouted the man.

The orderlies pulled another chain and the vent closed. Another ran over to Vincent with fire extinguisher and put out his burning body. He continued to writhe and scream even after the flames were out. Every inch of him was agony.

"Take him to his cell and feed him. I need him alive. He is more important than I realised," said the man.

The orderlies wheeled Vincent back to his cell. They pushed the tube down his throat again and pumped blood into his stomach. The man pulled off his gloves, mask, and apron as he ran out of the operating theatre and into the corridor. He fished his phone from his pocket, selected a name from his contact list, and pressed dial.

"Hello. I need to speak to Mr. Saltorg right now please?" he said.

"I'm sorry, Mr. Saltorg is in a meeting at the moment," said the PA on the other end of the line.

"This is Doctor Revitska. Mr. Saltorg, I need to talk to him right now, please," the man said.

"And I said he is in an important meeting," said the PA.

"Listen to me and listen well. I'm Dr. Revitska. Head surgeon of Medicyber Medical technologies. I don't care how important Mr. Saltorg's meeting is, pull him out of it right now! I have information that is vastly more important to him than any other matter could possibly be. Do not underestimate me, I am not someone who you should disappoint. I have connections everywhere who can make you disappear before this day is through. All I have to do is say the word. So you see, it is in your best interest to put me through to him this instant," said Revitska.

"I'm sorry, please forgive my ignorance. If you could kindly hold the line for one moment," said the PA in a startled voice.

A hold tone beeped a few times into Revitska's ear, then the deep, vaguely European accented voice of Saltorg came down the line.

"Dr. Revitska, there better be an incredibly good

reason for this call. You have pulled me out of a videoconference with all my investors and shareholders. Now, what could possibly be so important?"

"Did Lord Ruhsarr ever give anyone else the dragon's blood but you and your brother and sisters?" said Revitska

"No, you know how the story goes. Each of the brothers and sisters were fed the dragon's blood. Later Lord Ruhsarr drank what remained. There are no others who drank the dragon's blood. What is this about?" said Saltorg in a stern tone.

"I have a prisoner from whom I have been trying to extract information. He's a vampire but Lady Gilad believes he is a traitor who is working with Andra Hudson. You remember, that S.O.V.E.U. bitch. Anyway, we exposed him to sunlight but he didn't burn, not straight away anyway. It took a full five minutes for him to ignite and even then he burned at a slow rate," said Revitska.

"What? That's impossible! The only way he could resist fire for that amount of time was if he had drank from the dragon's vase," Saltorg said but then fell quiet as he thought about that for a moment. "The only other way he could resist the sun for so long is if he was one of the...the…"

"One of the two prophesised sons of a pregnant woman bitten by Lord Ruhsarr," said Revitska.

"Lord Ruhsarr has been expecting them to show up sometime soon. But he's always talked about such people, even since the beginning. Assuming he is who we think he is, is it possible we could find the human brother with this prisoner of ours?" said Saltorg.

"This prisoner of mine. I want full credit for my work," said Revitska.

"The prisoner belongs to me and the other members of The Children of the Blood. It will do you well to remember whom you work for, doctor," snapped Saltorg.

"Yes sir, sorry sir, I'm just very passionate about this," said Revitska then fell silent for a moment. "In answer to your question, it is just a matter of time. We will torture him more when he's healed."

"There is another way Doctor," said Saltorg.

"That way has worked in the past, sir, but it is a path with no return. It would mean someone willingly sacrificing themselves," said Revitska.

"It would be for the greater good. They would be helping to eliminate the biggest threat our species has ever faced. It would make them a martyr. Plus the short-term benefits of vampiric cannibalism might appeal to some," said Saltorg.

"When you put it like that, I think I might have just the right candidate, sir," said Revitska.

"Good. Get all the preparations in order and I will be there in one hour. Give this prisoner some human blood, not too much though. The prophecy says he will be the strongest of our kind to have ever lived," said Saltorg.

"I'll get those preparations underway, sir. As for the prophecy, I have not seen any evidence that he is stronger than any of the rest of us," said Revitska.

"Be careful anyway. Just because you haven't seen the evidence doesn't mean that the prophecy is wrong. Now, please excuse me. I need to close the meeting I was in and cancel the rest of today's appointments. See you soon Doctor," with that Saltorg hung up the phone.

Revitska ran to the block of cells and burst into the one in which Vincent was being held.

"Get the prisoner fed and prepped I want him in the operating theatre and ready for when Mr. Saltorg arrives!" he shouted.

"Mr. Saltorg is coming here?! When will he arrive?!" said an orderly who was tending to Vincent's wounds.

"In one hour," said Revitska.

"That isn't enough time, sir. He needs to heal," said another orderly.

"I don't want to hear excuses, I want you to get it done! Mr. Saltorg gets what Mr. Saltorg wants" said Revitska.

"Indeed, sir," they said and began to hurry around the room.

Vincent lay still on the table; only his chest rose and fell with each breath. He was conscious but every move he made sent horrendous pain through his entire body. The tube in his throat was filling him with blood and saving his life. It was helping his body to heal faster. Unfortunately, he was only being healed for the next round of torture.

Saltorg's helicopter landed on the helipad on the roof of the Medicyber HQ building. Dr. Revitska rushed over to greet him as he disembarked then led him down to the operating theatre.

"Please be seated, sir. Is there anything I can get you?" he said.

"Where is the prisoner?" said Saltorg impatiently as he took his seat.

"He's being prepared and will be brought in shortly," said Revitska.

"Good, and the volunteer?" said Saltorg.

"He's in a holding cell and will be along shortly too," said Revitska.

"Who is he?" said Saltorg.

"His name is Charles Hackett, sir. An old political prisoner. He says he will do just about anything to be freed. He's been told what he has to do and he will be granted his freedom on completion of the task. I have been experimenting with a serum to reverse the effects of the consumption of vampire blood. We should have about three hours before the effects are irreversible. He will be a good test subject," said Revitska.

"Ok, good job, Dr. It seems you have everything in hand. Please continue," said Saltorg with a genuine smile

"Thank you kindly, sir," Revitska clapped his hands. "Bring in the prisoner."

The orderlies rolled Vincent, still strapped to the same gurney, into the room. His flesh had healed somewhat, but he still had deep burns on some areas of his body.

"I thought you said he had been burnt. It looks like he was barely damaged," said Saltorg.

"He's healed quite substantially. Now you see what I meant when I talked to you on the phone. Any other vampire would have been ashes and dust but he was mildly burnt. We gave him blood to heal him in time for your arrival," said Revitska.

"Interesting. You may proceed," said Saltorg.

"Indeed sir. Please bring in our volunteer!" said Revitska.

An orderly led a tall, slender man into the room. He was clothed in a ragged old shirt and pants."

"Are you ready, Charles?" said Revitska.

"Yes. You will cure me and let me go when the task is done?" said Charles.

"Yes Charles, but remember, only feed a little then tell us what you see," said Revitska.

"Ok," said Charles. He turned to Vincent and whispered, "I'm sorry about this but I need to get back to my family."

Vincent didn't reply, he just glared back at Charles who tried to avoid making eye contact. He leaned forwards and wiped away a bit of ash from the crook of Vincent's elbow. He then opened his mouth and pressed his teeth onto the area and sunk them into the flesh. He let the blood only partially fill his mouth. He pulled away, turned to face the two superior vampires, and wiped his lips on his forearm.

"I see… a boy… in a house….47 Queen Street in Didcot. He's the one…the prophesised one!" he said as a look of dread grew on his face.

"Where is Andra?" said Revitska.

"She is... she is in..."

Charles threw his head back and screamed as a burning sensation rose in his throat. He felt every nerve ending in his body explode.

"Inject him with the serum! Quick he's about to come apart," yelled Revitska.

One of the orderlies picked up the syringe in an attempt to inject Charles but he couldn't keep hold of him. He thrashed with so much sudden strength that the orderly was thrown aside as if he were a rag doll. A scream gurgled from Charles' throat as red hot blood spurted from his nose and mouth. His eyes burst and plumes of ash were ejected from his face. He tore at his neck until the flesh came away in his hands. His chest lit up as his internal organs became an inferno. He threw his head back again and let out a scream of agony as a six foot flame shot from his mouth. His whole body burst into a bright blue flame. All the spectators ran for the doors as his burning husk stumbled around for a moment and then fell apart.

Revitska and Saltorg were the only two who remained seated with their mouths hung open in shock.

"What the fuck was that?!" said Saltorg.

"I must apologise Mr. Saltorg. I've seen the effects of vampire cannibalism before but I've never seen anyone react like that," said Revitska

"Oh well," said Saltorg. "He served his purpose. He will be remembered for generations if the boy is found where he said he is. Now, I need to make some calls. We will have that little bastard before tomorrow is done. Thank you Dr. Revitska. You may just have saved us as a species. In the meantime be careful what you do with this prisoner. If that's what his blood does who knows what the rest of him will do."

"Thank you too, Mr. Saltorg. The pleasure has been all mine," said Revitska.

"I will be in contact soon," said Saltorg with a smile. He stood up from his seat and walked back up through the building to the helipad. As he did he unlocked his phone, found Dienco in his contacts and pressed dial.

Chapter 28.

Alex had noticed Vincent was missing too. He missed talking with him and the CDs that Vincent would bring him. They were friends now as well as brothers as their experiences since their return from France had pulled them closer together.

He was training in the gym of the base while Andra sat and supervised him. He stopped on a platform after climbing a cargo net.

"Andra, when is Vincent coming to visit?" he said.

"I don't know yet. He's been very busy at the moment," she said.

"Last time I saw him he told me that he was working for you spying on vampires," he said.

"Yes, that's right. He's been reporting back and letting me know information that he has found out. He is doing good work for us. It's something not many people are brave enough to do," she said with a smile.

"You would tell me if something had happened to him wouldn't you?" he said.

"I knew you would have some intuition about him. All I know is that he hasn't checked in for the past few weeks but it's nothing to worry about. He might just be in deep with the vampires he is surveying and can't risk breaking character," she said.

She was worried about him though. It had been nearly three weeks and he hadn't so much as sent a text.

"Are you worried about him?" he said.
She closed the book she was reading and placed it down on the chair beside her.

"No. Vincent is capable of looking after himself. Are you worried?" she said.

"I always worry about him. Is that normal?" he said with a frown.

"Yes, that is perfectly normal. Worrying about your loved ones is what makes you human. Right, you're at the halfway mark now. I'm going to start coming around the course and I want you to try and beat me to the end," she said.

Alex laughed and started the climb across the next obstacle as Andra reached the first one. She went easy on him and let him win but her plan worked and it took his mind off his brother for a while. As the weeks became a month there was still no sign of Vincent.

Alex continued to do well at school and didn't get in any more trouble. He had noticed that as he walked through the corridors and in the playground all the other kids stayed a few feet away from him. They were scared of him since the fight. All of them but one boy called William Wentworth who thought of himself as the class bully. He approached Alex on Monday morning break.

"Hey Alex, I've got a plan. We could go around and tell the other kids that if they don't give us their sweets you will beat them up. No one is going to mess with you. Imagine all the sweets we could have," he said.

"No, I'm not going to scare people. I don't want their sweets anyway," said Alex.

"You're such a loser," said William.
Alex fixed him with a cold stare.

"I could beat you up and show them who the real loser is," said Alex.

"I…was…I was only joking, Alex. I don't want other

people's sweets either," said William.

"Good," said Alex and walked away.

When he got back to Roger and Sarah's house he told them what William had said.

"I don't want them to be scared of me," he said.

"Don't worry. Stay away from him and just concentrate on learning. The others have lost a bit of their trust in you. Keep working hard and show them that you are not a threat and they will start to trust you again," said Roger.

"You might find that there are kids like William who'll want to be your friend because you scare the other kids. Don't listen to those people though. If people only want you as a friend because they can get something from you or because you can help them bully other people without consequences they are not real friends," said Sarah. Little did he know then but the advice they gave him that day would stay with him for all his life. He loved them and the time he spent with his new family and they loved him.

A few days later Alex was staying at the Booth's house again. It was a quiet autumn night, all the family and Alex were all sleeping. He was suddenly pulled from a dream by a sound almost too quiet for humans to hear. It was the sound of something scraping across the roof tiles. He realised it was the sound of something landing on the roof of the house too. He got up and took his katana from its lockbox beneath his bed. He then ran to Roger and Sarah's room and shook them awake.

"Somethings landing on the roof," he whispered.

"What?" said Roger.

"There is something landing on the roof," he said. Roger pushed a panic button on the wall and he and Sarah got out of bed. They pulled open the bedside draws and opened the small gun lockers within. They each took out an Uzi 9mm and screwed suppressers to the end of the barrels of the guns.

"Stay quiet. Hopefully they don't know where we are within the house," Sarah whispered to Alex as she silently slid a magazine into her gun.

The sound of glass being smashed emanated and Mary screaming emanated from the room across the landing. Sarah quietly ran across the landing. Roger and Alex were quick to follow her. She swung the door wide open and shot a vampire who was trying to climb in through the broken window. It fell down to the back into the yard and shattered to dust as it hit the ground. Sarah gathered Mary up and ran to the landing. Two more vampires dressed in black combat gear and balaclavas quickly climbed through the window. Roger raised his gun and shot them. Another tore a hole in the roof and landed in front of Alex. He reached out a hand to grab the boy but Alex readied his katana.

"Aww did they give you an ickle sword?" said the vampire in a condescending tone.
Alex swung the blade and sliced off the vampires arm. He watched in shock as his arm shattered on the floor. Alex pushed the point of the blade through the vampire's heart.

Roger had woken Andrew and the family made their way down the stairs. They kept the vampires in place at the top of the stairs with short, well aimed, bursts of gunfire. Three vampires crashed through the front door so the family made their way down the hall. They moved into the kitchen at the back of the house. Shooting into the growing crowd as they made their way towards the back door. Roger had to change his mag, as he did a vampire leapt on him and clawed at his neck.

"Roger!" shouted Sarah and the kids screamed. Alex thrust his blade through the vampire's throat, while Sarah shot it five times in the chest and it fell to ash and slipped from the sword. Alex took Roger under the arms and dragged him back. Sarah continued to shoot at the vampires in the hall while more of them came down the stairs. Roger was keeping pressure on the wound but was still bleeding heavily. He was still able to shoot his gun though. One of the vampires burst into flames and ash as he shot it through the chest. The kids fumbled with the keys as they tried to unlock the back door as vampires moved closer and closer. One of them lunged forward and tried to stab Alex. Roger and Sarah shot it in the chest and head at the same time. Alex let go of roger and took the knife from the burning vampire's hand, then threw it into the crowd. The blade buried itself in the eye socket of another vampire. They thrashed around and knocked another vampire off balance. This one stumbled towards Alex who quickly took a step forwards and thrust his katana forwards. The blade pierced its heart and a moment later the vampire was ash. Sarah picked off more of the crowd as Roger stifled a cough. Alex leaned down and hooked his hands under his arm again.

"Leave me. I'm done," he said.

"No way," said Alex as he dragged him across the kitchen.

The kids finally unlocked the back door and opened it

slightly. Sarah slid through the gap while still holding her gun up in the direction of the vampires. She turned around and pointed her gun out into the night but saw nothing and no one outside. She looked back into the kitchen and gestured for the others to follow. More vampires came down the stairs and moved into the kitchen. The family made their way out into the garden. As Alex dragged Roger out into the garden a vampire dropped from the roof and landed with its feet on Roger's legs. He screamed in pain. It leered down at him and as he made eye contact with it. He could tell there was a smile on its face under the balaclava. He aimed his gun at its face and squeezed the trigger. As the bullets passed through the vampire's head it fell forwards. Alex shoved it aside. Its last breath hissed from its lips and it crumbled to ash when it hit the ground. More vampires dropped from the roof and landed between the family and the house. Roger cried out as Alex pulled him further across the garden and they all made their way to the gate. The three of them fought off the waves of vampires as they filled up the garden. A light came on in the neighbour's house as they were roused from sleep by the noise. Sarah realised that it may have been a mistake to have come outside as the vampires became a horde. Roger's gun clacked as the magazine ran empty.

"I'm out," he said.

"Me too," said Sarah as her last magazine ran dry.

"We need to move, we need to move now," said Alex and moved to open the gate.

A small silver cylinder flew over the fence with a 'pop'. It landed among the vampires and white gas spewed from it and began to form a cloud. They began to cough and choke as the gas ate their flesh. The gate splintered then was torn out from the fence and there dressed in her black, figure hugging, costume stood Andra.

"Go, get in the van," she said.

As they hurried past her she took Sarah by the arm, "You did well," she said.

"We got our arses kicked," said Sarah.

"You're all still breathing. That is enough," said Andra.

She then ushered them into the back of the van. Three balaclava-less vampires ran towards Andra snarling and growling. Without missing a beat she swung the long blade of her Monk's Spade at the first one. He was sliced in two at the waist. The next one raised a machete and swung it at her. She turned, stepped aside. The blade cut into her shoulder. She knocked their arm aside and jabbed the crescent moon blade into his midriff, spilling his entrails. She pulled the monk's spade back then flipped it over and split the vampire vertically down the middle. The last of the three saw how fast her purple flesh healed and the dexterity with which she had dispatched the other two. She turned and saw a look of realisation in his eyes. He knew who she was and tried to run. With effortless ease, she leapt towards him, pushed the blade through his back, and lifted him from the ground. His mouth opened as if to scream but a flame shot up from his throat as his internal organs burned. She shook his remains free of her blade. The van drove alongside her, she stepped inside and slid the door shut as they drove away. Soon sirens grew closer but the van was already a good distance away from the house. She started tending to Roger's wounds right there in the van.

"I'm sorry that I took so long. I'll take you directly to the medical unit the moment we get to base," she said.

"Don't apologise. We would have been dead if it wasn't for you," he said.

"You saved our lives," said Sarah.

Tears rolled down her face and the kids hugged her.

Alex sat with his head down and cried silent angry tears. This was the second family he had nearly lost because of the vampires. He felt the anger burn deep inside him while something else twist and knotted up. In the following years he would realise this feeling was hate.

Soon the van drove into the warehouse and parked in the garage. Andra had already radioed ahead so when she opened the back doors two of the medical staff were waiting with a gurney. They lifted Roger onto it and rushed him down to the medical bay. Sarah and the kids got out of the van.

"Are you ok?" said Andra.

"I feel a lot safer now we are here," said Sarah as she hugged the children. Andrew and Mary cried but Alex was seething with anger. He paced back and forth till Andra grabbed him and hugged him close.

"Alex, tell me how you feel," she said.

"Pissed off, pissed off is how I feel," he said.

"It's ok. You are allowed to be angry. Just remember not to hold onto it," she said.

He rested his head on her shoulder and cried.

Chapter 29.

The next few months were hard on everyone. Andra co-operated with the police through a human assistant posing as the Booth's lawyer. They spun a tale of home invasion and mistaken identity. The authorities and the local papers bought their story.

The ash from the dead vampires was tested by their forensic labs but they found it to be of an undeterminable origin.

Roger was healing well but he would never be able to work for Andra again. Six weeks later he and Sarah handed in their notice to Andra sighting ill health and trauma as the cause. They decided to move with the kids to Peru to be near Sarah's parents. With a sad smile Andra accepted their resignation and hugged them both.

Two weeks passed and brought with it the day of the family's flight. Andra and Alex took them to the airport. They were all stood outside the departures lounge. Andra was wearing human flesh coloured foundation and dark glasses. The other travellers were too busy with their cases and saying goodbye to their loved ones to notice Andra. She held Sarah's hands in hers.

"If you need anything at all don't hesitate to ask. I will always be just a phone call away," she said. Then turned to Roger, kissed him on the cheek and said, "The same goes for you. Rest your legs and heal well."

"Thank you so much for everything you have done for us," said Sarah. She turned to Alex.

"I know Andra will take great care of you but look after yourself too. We will see you again one day. I just need some time with my family. We will miss you and will call you on the phone every day," she said. Roger slapped a hand on his shoulder.

"You will do well Alex. Andra is a good leader. She will teach you well," he said.

Mary and Andrew both hugged him at the same time.

"I'll miss you. See you soon," Mary said, her face wet with tears.

"I will miss you all too. I hope you have a nice time with your family," he said as his voice began to choke in his throat.

Sarah grabbed him and hugged him tight as the tears spilled from his eyes. She kissed him on the cheek and then hugged Andra. More teary goodbyes were said as they walked through the gate with their cases.

After the plane had departed Andra led Alex back to the car. As she drove they talked.

"We need to talk about Vincent," she said.

"I know," said Alex quietly with a frown on his face.

"We have to consider the possibility that he told other vampires where you were living," she said.

"I don't want to believe that," he said.

"I know, I can understand that. We can't just ignore the fact the vampires found you though. They came straight to the house, you were in serious danger. Don't you think it's strange that Vincent goes missing and one month later vampires attack you?"

"I think it's a coincidence but I don't think he'd do that to me," he said.

"He left you behind before, what would stop him doing it again?" she said.

"He might have been abducted and forced to tell them against his will," he said.

"Come on Alex. Don't be so naïve. You're smarter than that," she said.

"It's not Vincent who told them where we were. I have to believe that. If he had left of his own accord and told someone where I was they would have come for me sooner," he said.

"Alex, the vampires want you dead. They're not going to catch you or lock you up; they want to kill you. The chances that Vincent gave them that information are too high to just dismiss; even that was under the influence of torture. How can you still just say that it wasn't him?" she said.

"Because I have to believe it. Even if I am wrong and being naïve, I don't care. He's the only family I have left. Yes, he left before but then he came back. He gave up a whole new family of vampires, a family of his own kind, to save me. The woman he loved died and he didn't abandon me. I can't just turn my back on him. I have to believe in him. Even if I am the only one who trusts him. I am his brother and he would do the same for me," he said.

Andra looked at him and saw tears roll down his face.

"Ok, Alex. If you still trust him that is fine by me," she said.

They talked about Vincent many times in the next few years. Alex never gave in, he never gave up hope that his brother was still alive and that he would never give any vampires any information about him.

Chapter 30.

Time moved on as it inevitably does and so the years passed. The S.O.V.E.U. continued to raid vampire hideouts in an attempt to locate Ruhsarr. They knew that he wasn't in the U.K. and that they could not physically fight him. But if they could find intelligence about him and his location they could try to predict his next move. Those raids now extended to a search and rescue mission into the whereabouts of Vincent. Both searches went fruitless aside from rumours and speculation.

Most of the things that they discovered, besides some new vampire weaponry, were useless. They stole a high powered needle gun among other things with the intention of reverse engineering them. They found drugs specifically designed for vampire consumption. These were usually mostly useless on humans and served little in the way of medicinal benefits. They stole them anyway.

They discovered some werewolf dens but they were always empty. Werewolves usually keep themselves to themselves and only group together in times of great need. They caused very few problems for the S.O.V.E.U. these days. And although they had a violent and blood soaked history with vampires they rarely fought these days since both species had agreed to sign a treaty. This treaty stated that vampires and werewolves would not attack each other in their most vulnerable states.

After Alex and the Booth family had been attacked Andra gave up trying to help him have a normal life. She hired lectures to educate him in common school curriculums. He spent four days a week with a different S.O.V.E.U. member to learn everything else that lectures couldn't teach him. He enjoyed the physical fitness training the most. He liked to run the assault course with the new recruits and also had the physical speed and strength to play rugby with the soldiers. Sergeant Major Fletcher taught him lessons about science that went far beyond the curriculum parameters of any school.

Chapter 31.

August 2011.

Alex regularly found himself unable to sleep. He was sixteen now and mostly took care of himself. One night he got up from his bed, put on his slippers. He then made his way into the main kitchen to get a glass of water and see if there was anyone to talk to. A few soldiers working the night shift on their dinner breaks and in the far corner sat Andra. As he approached she looked up from the book she was reading and smiled warmly.

"Any good?" he said, making small talk.

"It's ok. It's about modern computer science. I've got to keep in the loop with these things," she said.

"It must be weird living for thousands of years with no computers and now they are everywhere," he said.

"A lot of modern technology is weird to me. Cars, planes, television sets," she said.

"You do know no one calls them television sets anymore?" he said with a smile.

"I am aware of this, I like it though. It sounds nice. TV is too…clean, too flashy.
There has always been new technology in one way or another. New inventions that have revolutionised the world. I remember the first time I saw glass," she said.

"Glass?" said Alex furrowing his brow.

"Yes, it's everywhere these days. Literally in everything. So much so that you don't notice. It's just another thing to you. When I first saw it I thought it was ice or some sort of mineral. It wasn't as refined back then, it had a lot of impurities, and as a result wasn't as clear as it now. I also remember the first time I saw members of the Roman Empire," she said.

"You met Romans?" he said.

"I did. They didn't like me," she said with a smile. "They tried to capture me as they thought I was the spawn of Pluto," she said.

"What did you do?" he said.

"I educated them in the ways of martial arts," she said and laughed.

"Is there anything you miss about the past?" he said.

"Yes. I miss a lot of things. Mainly I miss people the same as any human does. People like Myu Msyanto, Taki Usatsuh, Ranu Juhati and Tsang Huhatsui. They taught me everything I know about martial arts and the flow of life. Although it was a long time ago I sometimes miss being human. I also miss my husband," she said.

"You had a husband?" said Alex as he screwed up his nose.

"Don't look so disbelieving. I was married once… a long time ago now," she said.

"Sorry I didn't mean to come across as doubtful. You're just so independent I didn't think you were the marrying type," he said.

"We all need companionship. Besides, it was when I was human. They were different times," as she spoke she broke eye contact with Alex and had a faraway look in her eyes as the memories played out in her mind.

"What was he like?" said Alex.

"He was a good farmer, and a great man. He was also wonderful, and loving. I miss his long, blonde hair and his blue eyes. I still remember those eyes, so handsome," she smiled to herself.

"What happened to him?" said Alex.

Andra looked down at her hands as if she was about to cry but when she looked up she looked strong and defiant.

"Ruhsarr, that fucking arsehole, killed him before he turned me into…this," she said.

"That's why you hate him?" he said.

"Yes, he took my husband, and then he took my humanity," she said.

"Did you know Ruhsarr back then?" he said.

"Yes. He was a good man a long time ago. He owned the farm in the next valley from ours. A dragon took a liking to a cave on his land. We all told him to abandon the land. Instead, he tried to kill the dragon but it bit him. Its venom twisted his mind and his body turning him into the monster he is today," she said.

"And I'm going to destroy him?" he said.

"That is what the prophecy says," she said.

"But how, he's a monster?" he said.

"Alex, listen to me. History is filled with stories of the small and the weak defeating the mighty. You will find a way, you have to believe in yourself. I believe in you. This is the hand fate has dealt you, you have to play it. You will play it and you will win," she said.

"Ok," he said.

"Say, yes Ma'am," she said.

"What?" he said.

"Say, yes Ma'am," she said.

"Yes ma'am," he said.

"Good, now go back to bed and get some sleep," she said.

"Yes ma'am. Good night," he said and smiled.

"Good night, Alex," she said and smiled back at him, before returning to her book.

Chapter 32.

March 2013.

The vampires had been quiet for a while and things seemed to have settled down a little. That was until an unmarked S.O.V.E.U. van was driving through the streets of Sunderland at 4 pm on an innocuous Tuesday afternoon.

Major Foster, Sergeant Jones, and Corporal Wells were just returning to the local base after getting food for themselves and some other soldiers. They were stopped at a traffic light when a motorbike with a rider and a passenger pulled up on the other side of the street from them. They were dressed all in black protective gear and had UV protective visors in their helmets. The Soldiers in the van thought nothing of it until the rider of the bike drew a submachine gun and opened fire on them.

"What the fuck!" shouted Sergeant Jones from the back of the van.

"Return fire," said Major Foster from the driver's seat. Jones and Wells slid open the panels on the side of the van and pointed out the barrels of their M16s. They let off a few rounds when the passenger of the bike raised what looked like a poster storage tube. The soldier in the van were confused until an RPG shot through the open panel and into Jones' face. It exploded with the same force as a tank buster causing damage similar to placing a firework inside a tin can. The soldiers inside were vaporised.

Andra was sat at the computer in her office in Base 107 when Sergeant Collins ran into the room.

"Ma'am, one of our vans has been attacked in Sunderland. It's all over the news," she said.

"Today?" said Andra.

"Yes ma'am. About twenty minutes ago," said Collins.

"Ah shit!" said Andra as she switched on the TV and found a news channel.

The female news reporter stood on a street that had been cordoned off with police tape and in the background smoking remains of the van were scattered all over the road.

"The attack happened just after four pm. Eyewitnesses say that two motorcycle passengers shot what is thought to be some kind of rocket propelled grenade into an unmarked police vehicle. No terrorist organisation has yet taken responsibility for the unprovoked attack. The three occupants of the van were killed instantly and many more were injured. People here are shocked…" The reporter was cut off as Andra clicked the power button.

"Fucking twats. I need to make some phone calls," she said.

"Yes, ma'am said Collins and walked away.

Two weeks later another van and its occupants were destroyed in a similar fashion. The S.O.V.E.U. soon became aware of this strategy and equipped all the vehicles with silver laced tear gas grenade launchers. In turn, the vampires started wearing gas masks and airtight suits. So the vans were fitted with flame throwers. Every attack the vampires attempted in that time was quashed until they began wearing flame retardant clothing. This resulted in Andra calling a meeting with Commanding Officers from her other regional headquarters.

"These attacks are turning from skirmishes into gangland warfare with all out guerrilla tactics. We are drawing far too much attention to ourselves," she said.

"For every vampire hideout we take they destroy one of our bases. They are gaining ground faster than we can take it and their numbers are rising sharper than they ever have," said O'Brien.

"Ma'am, our numbers are falling fast. We have lost bases in Liverpool, Blackpool, Devon, Sunderland, and Essex. These are strategic areas we have held for centuries" said Edmund.

"The technology the vampires were using is more advanced than any we have ever seen from them. I want to know where they are getting the funds for these weapons," said Andra.

"Ma'am, I think I speak for everyone when I say we need an edge otherwise they are going to wipe us out," said Thomas.

Chapter 33.

By the age of nineteen Alex had learned all he needed from the staff of the S.O.V.E.U. to complete exams in accordance with the national curriculum. He decided to take Open University degree courses in English and Biology. He took the exams and got 1:2 degrees in both. After that he and Andra decided it was time that he began military training.

"If I'm going to be this weapon against the vampires I have to know how to fight," he said.

"And fight well," added Andra. "You will have to be efficient and deadly. The best you can possibly be."

"I agree," he said.

"I remember when your dad first asked me to train him. I told him that his training would start at 9 am. Your training will start earlier," she said.

"When you say earlier what do you mean?" he said.

"Earlier," she said with an evil smile.

The moon was low in the sky and Alex was stood in waist high grass looking out across the field as the blades shimmered and waved in a subtle breeze. He saw an area of movement of a different kind to his left and turned his head to track it. As he did huge snarling tiger burst forth and landed on him. He fell to the ground with its jaws inches away from his face.

"Get up soldier. On your feet now!" it shouted in Andra's voice.
A sense of shock crashed over his body like a tidal wave and he began to realise this was a dream

"Uh? Who are... what's going on?" he said.

"I said get up soldier!" he heard Andra say again.

"What the hell, Andra?" he said as he opened his eyes then squinted them almost shut again. The red digits of the clock on his bedside cabinet shone brightly at him. "It's 4.30 am!"

"Yes, it is. This is the first real day of your training as we agreed, so get out of bed. I'm going to train you as a soldier and I expect you to act like a soldier," she said. He rolled over further under his duvet and groaned. He was lifted into the air and was then falling as she flipped his bed over and tipped him onto the floor.

"What the fuck, Andra?!" he said

"I said up, and don't you dare swear at your superior!" she snarled as she towered over him. "Now get to your feet and stand to attention."
He knew by now that Andra wasn't the type to be happy about having to ask twice. She also didn't need to get in your face to be intimidating. So he did as he was told.

"Yes ma'am," he said.

"Sorry, did you say something?" she said.

"Yes ma'am," he said.

"I can't hear you?" she said.

"Ma'am, yes ma'am!" he said.

"That's better. Now today we are going to work hard and train hard. Over the course of your training we are going to work on distance running, weight training, hand to hand combat, melee weapons, and small arms," she said.

"I can already use a sword and a gun," he said.

"I know you can wield a sword and fire a gun. Can you maintain a sword or strip down a gun, clean it and reassemble it back to functionality? Do you know a full technique in either?" she said.

"No Ma'am," he said.

"Well then, that is what you are going to learn," she said.

"Yes Ma'am," he said.

They descended in the lift down to the gym on the seventh floor Andra made him run six miles on the running track.

"This is easy," he said.

"In that case keep going until you are tired," Andra said.

He finally gave up after thirty miles. The weight training was hard going. All muscle groups, as heavy as he could stand for three sets of fifteen reps.

For the combat training she taught him some techniques and then kicked his arse. She repeated the process until he was using the technique and he could hold his own. But she left him in no doubt that she could beat him.

For small arms she took a pistol from her waistband. She held it up with her hand on the grip and rotated it to show off all its angles.

"This is a 1939 Mauser Luger. It is one of the most difficult weapons I have ever field stripped and cleaned. When you master this everything else will feel easy. Think of it as a puzzle," she said.

Three hours later he walked to the desk where she was sitting and placed the weapon on top of the open book she was reading. She picked it up, looked it over, , looked down the sights and pulled the trigger. With a satisfying click the hammer slid and shot back into place. She smiled and looked at him. He just frowned.

"This is crazy, it doesn't even fit together properly," he said.

"Do it again," she said and passed it back to him.

"But I..." he began in protest.

"Again!" she said and waved him away with her hand before returning to her book.

An hour and a half later he came back with the gun and she looked it over.

"Again," she said.

Forty five minutes later he came back.

"Good, do it again," she said.

"Again?!" he said.

She shot him a look that could have killed a lesser person. He stormed off and came back with the gun ten minutes later.

"Again," she said.

Another five minutes later he came back with the gun. She looked at him and opened her mouth to speak but he spoke first.

"If you say again one more time you can clean this fucking thing yourself! My eyes sting and my fingers hurt."

"I was about to say well done. Most people take many hours just to learn to clean one of these. Some people simply can't. Why do you think armies across Europe stopped using them? You have just done, in five minutes, what others continually struggle with. You should be proud of yourself," she said.

"Ok... I'm sorry, I am... Thank you for training me," he said.

"You're welcome. Now go and rest. You have more training tomorrow," she said.

As he got into his bed that night and was asleep before his head touched the pillow.

His training continued for four months. He would train all week then and have weekends to rest. She pushed him harder than any normal recruit in everything she taught him, and he soaked it all up like a sponge. His mind was human with dormant vampiric DNA. This caused him to have the curiosity of a human and the learning speed of a vampire. His physical attributes benefitted from the training too as his muscle mass grew and his agility increased even further.

"Your strength is building at an incredible rate. You're about three times as strong as most people your size. Your speed and agility are beyond that of any of my soldiers."

"Still not strong enough to fight Ruhsarr though," he said.

"Nope, not yet," she said.

"So what do we do?" he said.

"We keep training. You're going to be a fucking beast," she said with a smile.

Andra set up an assault course for him to run alongside some of her soldiers. These were strong, intelligent people who had trained for many years and were at the top of their game but he outdid them at every level. He ran this twenty minute assault course in a little over seventeen minutes. A few days later she had devised an assault course that would challenge him. It had fifty feet high cargo nets, twelve feet high vertical walls, ninety foot climbing walls, and forty feet long balance beams.

After a few runs his fastest time was twenty eight minutes. Fifteen other soldiers completed it in forty minutes. The only person to get around it quicker than him was Andra herself.

Alex appreciated all the things that she provided for him but like his brother, he began to get the urge to spread his wings. Soon he started to sneak out in the mornings as the sun rose. He was quiet and fast as he ran through the streets to his old school. He would climb the side of the building then run along to rooftop and jump to the next rooftop. There was a distance of fifteen feet between each of the first three buildings and he could clear them by a few extra feet. The gap to the last building was twenty feet. He tried to attempt it once and lost his nerve at the last moment. This time he was determined that he was going to do it. He calmed himself and took a deep breath then got himself ready and pictured himself landing on the next building.

"Come on, Alex. You know you can do this," he said aloud to himself.

He set off running, got up to speed, and jumped. He landed only his toes on the very edge of the rooftop. He flailed his arms and looked over his shoulder. The thirty foot drop looked a hell of a lot higher from up here. He tried to catch his balance but try as he might he couldn't keep from falling back. His mind raced. What would he tell Andra? Would he survive the fall? Just as he was about to plummet to the ground below a hand grabbed his arm and dragged him roughly back onto the roof.

"Oh, thank god, you saved me…erm...why are you here?" he said.

"Why am I here!? Why the hell are you here!? What

the fuck are you playing at!?" said Andra in her sternest voice.

"I'm just practicing. If I'm gonna be hunting vampires it'll be places like this that I'll be doing that," he said.

"And what if you had fallen!?" she said.

"I would have been hurt," he said with a frown.

"Yes, yes you would! You have to be careful, Alex. A vampire could take a fall from this height in their stride. If you fall from this height you could be killed," she said.

"I know ma'am but you can't wrap me in bubble wrap all my life until I become this hunter of vampires," he said.

"I'm not wrapping you in bubble wrap. I'm just advising you," she said.

"I know. I… I didn't mean it in a derogatory way. I just meant you've got to allow me to make some mistakes," he said.

"I get it, you need some space. That's understandable," she looked him in the eyes and gave him a sly smile. "Tell you what, I'll let you off…if you can beat me in a race. From here to the centre of town then back home." He smiled back at her "Sure, try and keep up…if you can," he said and set off running.

She kept up with him just fine, she even let him lead for a while then sped past him with a smile and a wave. This run became part of the training and it was fun for them both. They made up their own game where they would get as close to people as possible without being seen.

Almost a year and a half later they were in the gym.

They had been running on the rooftops and when they got back to the base Alex ran another twenty miles.

"Ok, Alex. Combat," she said and passed him his katana while she took up her monk's spade.

"Try to get in close. Today's objective is to attack me if you can with the prime areas being the head and the chest. Semi-contact though if we can help it because you don't want to die and I don't want any wounds; I have an important meeting this afternoon. Freestyle defence and attack, all techniques and disciplines allowed. Good luck kiddo. Oh, and remember, you won't beat me but I want you to try," she said.

"Yes Ma'am," he said loud and clear.

"Begin," she said.

They circled each other for a minute as they watched one and others movements for tells. Andra made a few dummy moves trying to get him to react. Her first real attack came fast and without any warning. One second she was crouching, circling, the next the blade end of her monk's spade was slicing the air towards Alex's legs. He quickly blocked her blade with a downward swipe of his katana, then countered with an upward swipe towards her face. She stepped back then came forward at him swinging the crescent end towards his legs. He jumped over the blade and ran back a few steps then retook his stance. They continued circling each other attacking and defending. He ran at her as he swung his sword. She swung the blade end of her monk's spade towards him but he blocked it then leapt at her with his sword back and ready. She stepped in and head butted him. He fell to the floor, scrambled back to his feet, readied himself, and came back at her. Her blade sliced the air at waist height but he knocked it away. She swung the crescent end towards him but he ducked under it. She turned the blade over and brought it at speed towards his legs. After a swift block he then launched himself at her with is blade ready to jab towards her chest. She looked him in the eye then winked and leapt over him in a front flip. He lunged forwards, landed heavily, and slid across the floor. She landed effortlessly behind him and then turned to face him. Feeling humiliated, he jumped to his feet, and readied his sword. Anger burned in his eyes and contorted his face.

"Focus. Don't let anger lead your hand. Your technique will be sloppy and you will make mistakes that will get you killed. Use its power but control its flow," she said. He listened to her words and learned his lesson. He relaxed, centred himself, and took his stance. She took a stance then came at him. She threw punches and swung her monk's spade at him. He blocked and dodged but they were both just going through the motions. Now came her real attack as her blade sliced the air towards his head. He ducked just in time to hear it hiss inches above his scalp. She turned it in her hands and directed the blade down towards his right shoulder but he rolled to the left. She turned it again and the blade sped toward his legs but he jumped over it. She flipped the blade over and swung it back at him. He ran towards her and she back flipped away from him and landed. He then leapt into the air and kicked her in the chest. The attack caused her to take just one step back, so she ducked and swept his legs from under him before he landed. He hit the floor on his side with a heavy thud. He was quick to get back on his feet and shook off the pain in his knee and elbow. A moment later he ran at her. She threw attacks at him but he dodged every move she made. He jumped towards her then swung his sword past her face with the blade pointed back towards himself and clipped the tip of her nose with the pommel. He landed and ran away across the floor. She took the bait and chased him. He ran into the corner of the room then ran up the wall. She stopped for a second and looked up at him in awe as she realised she hadn't taught him this manoeuvre. That was the one moment of her broken focus that he needed. He leapt from the wall and back flipped over her head. She moved her monk's spade in his direction but he swung his sword with such force that he knocked the weapon out of her hands. It clattered across the floor as he landed behind her. As he did he wrapped his left arm around her neck and pressed the tip of his blade into her back aiming for her heart.

"If you were a vampire you would be dead now. Do you yield?" he said.

"I yield," she said and held up her hands.
He released his grip and she turned and bowed to him. He respectfully returned the gesture.

"You beat me. I've not been beaten by a human in a fight in nearly four thousand years," she said.

"In your defence, ma'am, I'm no ordinary human," he said.

"All the same, you have learned well, Alex. You are now a master. There is nothing more I can teach you about defending yourself besides technique," she said.

"Thank you, ma'am," he said.

"Thank you. Now go and rest. You've earned it," she said.

"Yes ma'am. Thank you ma'am," he said

Chapter 34.

March 2016.

Alex was standing in Andra's office. She walked in and handed him a Kevlar bulletproof vest.

"That should fit," she said.

He took it and slipped it over his head then fastened straps at the waist. He looked at the emblem on the front. It bore the letters S.O.V.E.U. and depicted below them was a vampire's skull with the handle of a knife protruding from the top of it. He smiled as he felt a rush of pride from wearing it. Andra slapped him on the shoulder.

"How does it feel?" she said.

"It feels good," he said and nodded.

"You don't have to do this, you know that don't you?" she said.

"I know, but I want to. Training is all well and good but I need real experience. I'm sure about this," he said.

"Ok," she said. She looked into his eyes and saw that he was serious. "Let me introduce you to my personal attack team."

She led him to the garage, and stood next to a black Ford Transit van were six soldiers. Alex had seen them around the base but had not worked with them before.

"First up is Steven White. He's a former sniper specialist and rifleman in the English Army. He's deadly close up and even more so from a distance," said Andra. Steven had silver-blonde hair and pale skin. He looked at Alex and made the finger guns gesture.

"Next we have Helen Davis. She's my explosives

expert, formally from the US Army. If there is anything we need destroyed or disarmed, she is the one we talk to. The fact she still has all her fingers is testament to her proficiency in her field," said Andra.

Davis was of mixed Mexican-Jamaican heritage with light brown skin and bright blue eyes. She looked at Alex and smiled.

"Next up is Zarveya Hussain. Don't be deceived by her small stature. She's an expert in small arms and close quarters combat. Formally from India but she made a name for herself in the British army. When she gets up close you're in trouble," said Andra.

Alex thought she was cute with her small frame and small round face. When he looked into her eyes he could see she was a formidable soldier.

"The giant is George Hughes. He's formally of the S.B.S. If it's a weapon he can use it. Don't be deceived by his physical presence. He's as intelligent as he is huge," said Andra.

She tapped her fist against Hughes' chest and he gave her a lopsided smile. He was taller than Andra, heavily built, with a ruddy complexion, and a blonde buzz cut. He had a snub nose, a wide jaw, and a long scar down his left cheek.

"This is Adam Palmer, formally a US Navy Seal. He specialises in heavily armed tactical combat and is extremely dangerous to anyone he sees as an enemy. I'm glad he's on our side and not theirs," said Andra.

Palmer, although shorter than Hughes was still tall in his own right. He was handsome with dark brown skin, and light brown eyes. His shaven head and heavy build gave him an imposing physical presence. He looked at Alex and Nodded.

"And on the end is Lucy Mc'Ready. She is a former member of the S.A.S. She specialises in technological warfare and cyber infiltration. Also, her skills with a rifle are in the top 97% of all our applicants, making her an extremely competent soldier," said Andra.
Mc'Ready made eye contact with Alex and a smile played at the corner of her lips. She had long, red hair, pale skin, and a strong but feminine physique.
Lucy looked at Alex and he felt a smile grow on his face appear on his face.

"Ok soldiers, take a seat in the van," said Andra.
They all climbed into the vehicle, she climbed in after them and slide the door shut.

"Ok, let's go," she said to the driver.
He started the engine and drove from the car park and out onto the road. They drove north for half an hour until they came to a small town.

"This is a small size den with somewhere between five and ten vampires. You know the drill, we go in quick and quiet. Hopefully, they will be from a weak blood generation and all fucked up. Even if they are they will still be strong, so we hit them like a ton of fucking bricks. Tonight, you bunch of bad mother fuckers, we're going to kick ass and take names!" she said.

"Fuckin' A!" said all the soldiers.

"Fuckin' A!" said Alex.
They pulled over behind a generic looking office block. Andra threw open the back door, and they all followed her out in single file. In silence they drew up along the side of an old disused foundry. As they came to the entry door Andra held up her hand and clenched it into a fist.

At this signal the soldiers stopped and stood still. She then held up three fingers and closed each one down into her hand. When she had closed all the fingers into a fist she stepped infront of the door. She then raised her leg and kicked it off its hinges. The door land and slid across the dusty concrete floor and she followed it into the building. The soldiers filed in after her. The huge expansive room was dark and stank of death and blood. All the windows had been boarded up or hurriedly painted black. All the old machinery and structural supports were covered with layers of rust.

A vampire screamed as it leapt out at Andra but was quickly bisected at the chest by her monk's spade. She knocked its burning husk aside and kept moving. Alex followed close behind her as they made their way into the building. They all switched on their head mounted lights as they checked the shadows and corners. A vampire burst out from the already broken door of an office and ran in Alex's direction.

"This one is yours, Alex, just remember what I've taught you," said Andra.
This vampire was a six foot, well-built male and raged as he ran at Alex.

"I'm gonna fucking kill you, you fucking human shit stain," he roared.
He collided with Alex, knocked him off his feet, and landed on top of him. There was a brief struggle and the flash of a blade. Alex kicked the vampire away as his flesh burnt to ash. Andra put out her hand and helped Alex to his feet.

"Fuckin' hell!" he said.

"They're fast in open spaces aren't they," she said.

"Yes. I killed a few years ago but I've never seen them on open ground," he said.

"The trick is to shoot or attack where you think they will be about a one to two seconds before they get there," said Hughes in his Welsh accent.

"Thanks," said Alex.

"No problem, lad," said Hughes.

Alex was slightly intimidated by the soldier. His height, huge build, and scared face misrepresented the man's kind and intelligent personality. Like Andra had said, he was glad this man was on his side, he wouldn't even like to entertain the alternative.

They continued to move into the building. Mc'Ready, Palmer and Hughes shot six vampires dead between them. Twenty minutes later they had swept the building when Hussain noticed a trap door in the far corner of the building that seemed to fall shut of its own accord.

"Ma'am, over there. Something moved," she said.

"Yes, I heard it. What was it?" said Andra.

"A trap door, over there," said Hussain.

They made their way over the door and stood around it. Besides the sound of dripping water, the whole room was silent. Andra stepped forward, pulled open the door. Davis pulled the pin from a grenade and dropped it into the hole. Andra let the door slam back down and a moment later the ground shook beneath their feet. There was a moment of silence then the door burst open. Three vampires flew out from the opening and landed amongst the soldiers. One landed on either side of Alex. He assessed the situation in a split second and moved his sword into position. He then sliced one of them from the groin up towards its ribs in one fluid movement. He had intended to slice it straight up the middle and could almost hear Andra saying focus in his head. He rotated the blade a little and sliced up through its chest and out through its neck. He then turned to the vampire on the other side of him. Its jaw was hanging off and its skin was charred from shoulder to knee down the left side. It was also missing its entire left arm. It snarled and reached out for Alex with its remaining hand which he promptly sliced off. A look of terror rose on its face as he swept the blade towards its neck and cut off its head. More vampires appeared from the trap door to attack the soldiers. These were no ordinary soldiers though, they are Andra's own personal attack team. They took down these vampires with well-placed gunshots and melee attacks. Andra jumped down into the tunnel which she found to be empty and collapsed. She climbed out and looked at the soldiers.

"Well done team. I think that is all of them. One more sweep and we can go home," she said.

"Yes ma'am," they all said.

Alex felt good being part of a team. They had moved through the whole building again and found it to be entirely empty.

"Ok soldiers, let's get out of this shit hole. There are beers with your names on back at the base," said Andra.

As they made their way out of the building she clapped a hand against Alex's back.

"You did well tonight. You should be proud of yourself," she said.

"Thank you, ma'am," he said.

"What do you guys think?" she said.

"Yes, you held your own in there," said Palmer.

"You can fight by my side anytime," said Mc'Ready. Davis gave her a sly wink and there was an almost indiscernible smile between the two women.

They all got back in the van and drove back to the base. The beers Andra had promised went down well amongst the soldiers as they chatted and laughed in the canteen.

For his work Andra started to pay Alex a wage. He joined her and the S.O.V.E.U. on another twenty-two raids over the next two years. Hideouts began to appear across the country with more frequency. The more Alex encountered vampires the better he got at killing them. He could reduce a group of them to dust in minutes and became an extremely efficient assassin and warrior.

"What am I going to do? Wipe out the vampire plague one hideout at a time? It's not enough," he said to Andra while they were in a meeting.

"Don't be too hard on yourself. I know what you mean though. You are brilliant so please don't take this the wrong way, but it just seems like something is missing. The result of a dragon's curse is never as simple as a soldier with beyond human abilities. You're supposed to be able to kill Ruhsarr. Something even I couldn't do. Ruhsarr is a monster in every sense of the word. He is unimaginably strong and almost indestructible. Along with that, he is intelligent and cunning. He would have killed me if it wasn't for my healing abilities. He could destroy you without even raising an eyebrow. I feel like something needs to happen but I haven't figured out what it is. Not yet anyway," she said.

Chapter 35.

May 2018.

Alex and Andra were in the gym training and had stopped for a break

"I've been thinking, I would like some independence. I want to rent a flat," said Alex.

"No," said Andra.

"Come on. I've been saving half my wage each month. It would just be a small place not far from here. There is a new apartment development two minutes away,"

"I said no, Alex," she said.

"Why the fuck not?!" he said suddenly.

"First of all, remember to whom you are talking. Second, the threat to you out there is still extremely real. I've made too many mistakes and put you at risk far more than I ever should have done. There have been times you could have been killed. I can't take any more risks," she said.

"I'm not asking to move miles away. Just enough so I can have some privacy," he said.

"What is wrong with your quarters here?" she said.

"They're here. That's the thing. All the other soldiers get to go home when they're on leave but I am always here. I never get away," he said.

"I don't know, Alex. Are you sure this is a good idea?" she said.

"Yes. We'll install a state of the art security system. UV lights, movement trackers, heat sensors, and a communication system so I can get in touch with you at the press of a button. Also, I was trained by you. This isn't like when I was a kid. I can defend myself better than any one of your soldiers," he said.

Andra fixed him with a look. She squinted her eyes and pressed her lips together.

"If I say ok you do as I say. I want to have a response team able you react at a moment's notice without your request or approval. Also if I say this is over you move back in here without questioning my orders," she said.

"Yes, that is fine. I agree with that," he said.

"Good. Don't make me regret this," she said.

"I won't, ma'am. Thank you, ma'am," he said with a broad smile.

Andra helped him with the paperwork and legal side of things. Soon he started renting one of the flats he had mentioned. It was a two minute car journey from Base 107.

He furnished it with his possessions including his couch, TV, Bluetooth smart speaker, and games consoles from his quarters at the base. A full bookshelf took pride of place along one of the walls in the large square living room. He put posters and paintings on the walls. There was a kitchenette at the back of this room. A door in the left wall led to the single bedroom. His king size bed and a wardrobe full of jeans, band t-shirts, and trainers fit perfectly in here. Off from this room was an on-suite bathroom. All the doors were removed and replaced with half an inch thick plate steel doors. With the flick of a switch all the lightbulbs could be switched between the visible spectrum of light and UV light. Despite these modifications to the undiscerning eye it all looked just like a normal apartment. It took Alex a few weeks to settle in, but soon it felt like home.

Alex went to work in the warehouse every morning just after as the sun rose. As part of his employment when he wasn't on patrol he taught martial arts to the new recruits.

The vampire population had continued to grow steadily in numbers year on year so he was always busy.

Under Andra's instruction, Fletcher had the science department routinely test samples of Alex's blood and skin. In December 2020 when Alex turned twenty five they took more of these samples. To their astonishment they found that his cells now replicated themselves perfectly. There was no cell mutation and no D.N.A. degradation. Like Vincent and all born vampires, the aging process ended for him. Andra had warned him this might happen.

"What does this mean?" he asked.

"It means…well, it means like me and most vampires there is the potential for you to be immortal," said Andra.

"I don't like the thought of being like a vampire." He said.

Andra placed a warm hand on his shoulder.

"I didn't want to live forever either when I first realised that it was a possibility; certainly not like this. I wanted to be buried next to my mother, father, and brother but I have come to terms with the fact that will never happen. I learned to accept this state of being and take solace in understanding that it can be a gift. Gandhi said 'live as if you were to die tomorrow, learn as if you were to live forever.' You'll soon realise you have the time to learn everything this world has to offer. No other human can say that," she said.

"You always know the right thing to say," he said.

"I've had a lot of time to practice," she said with a smile.

As he looked at her now, he saw all her hidden beauty. Ruhsarr had taken so much from her but through her own determination she had gained more than she had ever lost.

Chapter 36.

Alex lived in the apartment for many years without any incidents. One night he was sat reading when there was a knock at the door. He put his bookmark on the page he was reading, closed the book, and put down on the couch. He walked to the front door and looked through the peephole. A man and woman stood outside. They looked like junkies to him. They were skinny with gaunt faces. Their clothes were worn out and their hair was unkempt.

"Can I help you?" said Alex in a friendly tone.

"We want to come in, mate. It's me, Dan," said the man in a jovial voice.

"Sorry, I don't know you. You might have the wrong place," said Alex.

"No, this is definitely this flat we want mate. We can smell you in there. Open up so we can have a little chat," said the man.

"That ain't gonna happen," said Alex.
He realised now that the pair were vampires. From the looks of them he could tell that their vampirism wasn't all that strong. Maybe three or four hundredth generation.

"If you don't let us in I'll kick my way in, and you don't want that, mate," said the man.

"You can try if you like," said Alex.

"Ok, if that's the way you want it, but don't say I didn't give you a fuckin' chance," said the male.
He then raised his leg then kicked his heel against the door. It rattled in its frame and then he kicked it again and again. On the sixth kick the door burst open. Alex

backed away from them as they both stepped inside in a slinky, threatening manner. The man approached Alex with a pointy toothed smile and a long steak knife in his hand. The woman started rooting through his bookshelf and throwing its contents onto the floor.

"You got somefin we want and we're takin it whether you like it or not," said the man.

"I don't have any money if that's what you were looking for," said Alex.

"No man. That ain't what we lookin' for," said the man.

"What about this then?" said Alex and held up a handheld vacuum cleaner.

"The fuck would we need that for?" said the man with a confused expression.

"It's not for you," said Alex. "It's for me to clean you up with."

"The fuck are you on about mate? You high or somefin?" said the man.

"No, mate. No, I'm fuckin' not," Alex said and shook his head.

He flipped a light switch on the wall with a casual upstroke of his left arm. The vampires screamed as lights switched to UV. Their skin bubbled and burned away. Their flesh began to dry out and then separate from their bones. Just before they began to burn Alex leaned in close and looked into the eyes of the man.

"Broke into the wrong fuckin' place this time didn't you…mate," he said.

Moments later they were nothing more than two body shaped mounds of ash. They hadn't even damaged the flooring. Alex switched the lights back to normal then switched on the appliance and vacuumed them up. When he had finished he took his phone from his pocket and rang Andra's number. After a few rings she answered.

"Hello," she said.

"Hello, Andra. I'm gonna need a new, stronger front door," he said.

"What's happened?!" she said.

"Some vampires kicked my door in," he said.

"Oh shit! Are you ok?" she said.

"Yes. Don't worry, I'm fine. Oh, by the way, the UV lights work really well," he said.

"Ok, sit tight. I'll send Mc'Ready and Palmer to stay on guard with you until we can fix it in the morning," she said.

"I'll be ok by my…" he said.

"No. I'm sending them," she said cutting him off midsentence.

"Yes ma'am," he said and hung up the phone. He was ok with this arrangement. Palmer Mc'Ready had some cool combat stories. He also found Mc'Ready attractive; though he was a bit too self-conscious to tell her to her face.

Chapter 37.

Friday 7th August 2026.

Vincent had no perception of the passage of time in his cell so the days merged into one. Soon he had no idea how many had passed. It could have been weeks or months or even years. Through all his confusion of being awake and sedated they still asked him the same questions. "Where is Andra? Where is Alex?" And all the while they continued to torture him. They had cut his limbs off so many times he had lost count. They had tried other methods too. They had cut out his tongue, gouged out his eyes, pulled out his teeth, crushed his limbs, and poured acid all over him. They still force fed him blood so he would heal but he was always defiant. He never let them in, he didn't even speak to them anymore. Nothing they could do would break him.

They had last tortured him two days ago. They had dissolved his hands in acid and then hacked off what was left of his arms with a saw. Still, he wouldn't talk to them. He just lay there and spat at them whenever they came close. He now sat in his cell strapped to the chair with the tube down his throat. Saliva dribbled from his mouth as his mind swam on the precipice of insanity. His upper arms had grown back but his forearms and hands had still not formed.

A noise outside his cell pulled him from his stupor. There were always noises outside his cell. The laughter and arguments of vampires. The mournful cries of humans as they pined for their loved ones or their screams of horror as they were fed upon. This sound was different though. One he had not heard for many years now. Vincent could have sworn it was the muffled crack of gunfire, the calls of panic and death cries as vampire flesh burned and shattered across concrete floors. His thoughts were still fuzzy but he forced his mind to grasp hold of the reality of the situation just beyond his cell.

'Has Andra found me? Has she come to save me?' he thought.

The sounds of gunfire were close now and the guards outside his cell shouted in a panic. They screamed and there was a heavy thud against his door which rattled it in its frame. Then a moment of silence before the door was unlocked and quickly opened. He saw the silhouette of a woman standing in the door. It was clear from her small stature that she wasn't Andra. She strode in with an air of confidence that made it clear she was well versed in combat. She slung the AA12 automatic shotgun, which was almost as big as her, over her shoulder and pulled out a combat knife.

"Vincent Austin?" she said in a Spanish accent.

He nodded his head and grunted.

She cut the straps that held him to the chair and carefully pulled the tube from his mouth.

"Can you stand?" she said.

"Yes," he said in a hoarse voice.

She helped him up and walked him to the door.

"Who are you? Why are you helping me?" he said.

"My name is Sapora. I'm helping you because the Vampiric Empire betrayed me. Threw me to the wolves, literally," she said.

"What do you mean?" he said.

"Jake, the son of the Alpha Chief Werewolf, Jahlob,

attacked me and my partner, Micheal. However, in the attack Michael killed Jake. Because Jake was in human form at the time, it was seen as a breach of the treaty. Our leader, Lord Boltat, sided against us and kicked us into the street so Jahlob could hunt us like wild game. For his betrayal I killed Lord Boltat and his entire clan. Now, I don't care if every vampire in the world dies," said Sapora.

"The feeling is mutual. I'm done with vampires," he said with a smile. "How do you know about me?"

"After I cut Boltat's head from his pathetic shoulders I had enough time to look through his secret intelligence files. Your file was classed as top secret. They know about you and your brother. Your file documented your current location. I figured freeing you would fuck things up for them, so I came to break you out," she said. Vincent looked at her and smiled despite his pain. They continued to talk as she helped him down the narrow corridor. Unbeknown to them a silent alarm had been triggered when she opened his cell door. As they walked they heard the sound of many pairs of boots all marching in their direction. He looked into her eyes. They were beautiful but no beauty remained within them. It had been chased away through years of fighting, killing, and betrayal.

"This shit is about the get crazy. I know you're the brother of the prophesised child, so I presume you know about the dragon's curse," she said.

"Yes, I've heard of it," he said.

"Good. We were all strictly instructed that if we were to ever intercept your brother not to bite him but simply kill him. So it doesn't take a genius to figure out that to complete the curse we must bite your brother. I don't know what will happen after that but I do know Ruhsarr wants to prevent that from happening. Somehow after that he will have the ability to destroy Ruhsarr and the vampire plague," she said.

At that moment forty guards rounded the corner infront of them and opened fire. She pushed him back into a doorway as she leapt into the one across from him.

"Ruhsarr's fall depends on us getting out of here," she shouted over the gunfire.

"I have a plan," he said as a smile grew on his face.

"Care to share," she said.

He held up the stumps of his arms then opened his mouth to bare his fangs and made a biting motion.

"No way! That's suicide," she said with a look of horror on her face.

"It's the only way. My arms will grow back and it will give me the strength I need to get us out," he said.

"The years of torture have fucked your brain. It won't work," she said.

"There is only one way to find out," he said.

He flashed a smile and ran out from the doorway. Bullets tore at his flesh but he kept running. He jumped on the nearest guard, knocked him to the ground and bit into their neck without any hesitation. Blood squirted from the wound and filled Vincent's mouth. He swallowed it down until it stopped flowing. He stood up with bloody saliva dripping from his lips. He then threw his head back and let out a roar so loud it drowned out the gunfire. He flexed the muscles in his arms, and in a matter of seconds bones, tendons and ligaments pushed out from the stumps. Layers of muscle and flesh wrapped around them as more bones and grew from the stumps. A few moments later he flexed his new hands. Although bullets still tore at his flesh the wounds healed instantaneously. He grabbed another vampire and drained him of blood, then another. When his thirst was sated a rage sped through his body like nothing he had ever felt. The guards attacked him but he tore into them, pulling off limbs and cracking open skulls with ease. Sapora ran after him, she jumped over the broken vampires Vincent had fed upon. The bodies now burned and twisted as his vampire strain simultaneously changed and destroyed their flesh. The rhythmic boom of her shotgun filled the air as she picked off the vampires Vincent had only wounded. They burned up as the silver shots ripped through them. After a few minutes only Vincent and Sapora stood in the corridor. There was nothing left of the vampire guards but ash and dust.

"Now we definitely have to get out of here before more of them arrive," she said.

"Don't worry. I know a quick way out," he said.

"Good, let's go," she said.

He ran to a wall where a window had been bricked up and punched his hand right through it. Another few punches and he was stood looking out across the skyline of Birmingham. He looked down over the edge of the early nineteenth century building. Below them was a huge courtyard with adequate parking for articulated lorries. Its perimeter was surrounded by a high wire fence. Sapora stood next to him looking out.

"Do you think you could make that jump?" he said. She looked to the ground thoughtfully.

"Easy. It's only about ninety feet I'd say," she said.

"I mean over the fence," he said.

"That's impossible, even for us. I mean you could do it with a run-up but not from standing," she said. Without warning he grabbed her by the waist, lifted her up, and put her over his shoulder.

"Hey! What the hell!?" she said.

Before she could protest anymore he leapt. They sailed high into the air then came down and landed on the road twenty feet beyond the fence. The vampires inside the fence stood and looked at them in silent awe. Slowly they raised their guns and began to shoot at them. The engine of a black unmarked van roared as it sped along the road towards them. Vincent ran directly at it, and in response it sped up. Just as they were about to collide he slammed his fists down onto the bonnet. As its front suspension collapsed and the rear wheels lifted from the ground he grabbed the front of its chassis and threw it into the air. It flipped over him and crashed down behind him on its side. Its momentum caused it to slide along the road. The metal bodywork threw out sparks as it ground against the tarmac. Sapora shot the fuel tank on its exposed underside. It ruptured and drenched the vehicle and its occupants with petrol. Sparks hit the fuel and the whole thing burst into flames as it smashed into the fence and blocked the gate. The windscreen was kicked out and burning occupants staggered from the wreck. Their screams echoed across the courtyard as they twisted and writhed before their bodies exploded.

"That is definitely our cue to get the fuck out of here," she said.

"I know where my brother is. I can sense him, in here," he said and pressed two fingers of his right hand to his temple. "Are you coming with me?" he said.

"No, we should split up. I'll try to draw their attention while you escape," she said.

"I don't know how to thank you. Just saying it doesn't seem enough," he said.

"Find you brother and fulfill the prophecy…for all our sakes. That will be more than enough," she said.

"Will I see you again?" he said.

"I don't know, maybe," she said with a smile.
Vincent smiled and nodded then set off into a powerful sprint like a freed wild dog. He ran as no vampire had ever run before. He bound across the land reaching incredible speeds as the darkness enveloped him and sheltered him from human eyes.

'No vampire will ever catch me,' he thought.
And if it was for normal circumstances they wouldn't have either. Except, there was something giving away his position. Unbeknownst to him while he was unconscious Dr. Revitska had implanted a tiny transmitter chip at the base of his skull.

Chapter 38.

On Friday afternoon Alex had been sunbathing in the local park with Mc'Ready, White, and Davis. They were enjoying some downtime and the last days of summer. They all shared stories of their times in combat; both good times and bad. They all listened and supported each other. They had all finally said their goodbyes for the day at 11 pm. It was now 12.26 am, Alex was sat in his living room watching an old horror movie and drinking beer. He had already drunk one and had just opened a fresh one. As he poured it into his glass he heard a heavy knock on the apartment door.

After the incident with the two vampires breaking in a few years before he had fitted a solid two inch thick steel door with a multi-locking system. It also had a silent alarm that connected directly to the warehouse base. It was set to go off if the door was forced open or left open for too long.

He paused the film and put down the glass. As he entered the hall he took the M9 handgun from his holster that hung from the coat rack. He had just reached the door when there was another knock. He looked through the peephole and what he saw shocked him so much he had to step back from the door.

The person on the other side was his double except for his long hair and pale complexion. He raised his hand to the lock but then hesitated as hundreds of thoughts ran through his head.

'How is this possible? This must be some kind of trick. He can't be here. Have I been right all these years?'

He took a breath and opened the door just enough for him to look out with one eye. He held the gun just out of sight so if the person did try to force the door open he would be ready to pull the trigger.

"Hello, Alex," said Vincent.

Alex looked at this man's face. Was it really his brother? It was like looking in a mirror except for his eyes. They looked old and world-weary. The eyes of a person who had seen many indescribable horrors.

He opened the door fully and pointed the gun right at Vincent's face.

"Are you here alone?" he said.

"Yes. What the hell is are you doing? Is this how you greet your brother?" said Vincent.

"Damn right this is how I greet you. You disappear and a month later the family that I was living with got attacked. I hear nothing from you for over twenty years and you just turn up on my doorstep in the middle of the night. Did you expect me to welcome you with open arms?" said Alex.

"Twenty years? I knew I had been there for a while but… Is that really how long it has been?" said Vincent as a look of shock grew on his face.

"Yep," said Alex.

"I, er…I can explain everything but I don't have much time. I'm sorry you got attacked, honestly, I had nothing to do with that. I was captured by the vampires. They tortured me for years, Alex. All the time I've been gone they did horrendous things to me, but I never gave you up; not once. I could never give you up. You're my brother. You're my family," said Vincent.

Alex gave him a cold, hard stare. He thought about all

the things that had happened and that Vincent had left him before. He also remembered that Vincent had saved his life at the expense of his friends. He shook his head to himself.

"You've got a fucking lot of explaining to do. You better come in," he said and gestured towards the living room with the gun.

"Thank you, mate," said Vincent.

"Don't be so quick to thank me. Just because I've let you in doesn't mean I trust you. Go in and sit down," said Alex.

Vincent walked into the room in tentative manner like a caged animal released back into the wild. He slowly eased himself down on the sofa and looked around nervously like he expected to be accosted at any moment. Alex kept the gun in his hand. This man may have been his brother but he didn't like or trust Vampires. Even though he had trusted Vincent all those years ago, and had still hoped that he hadn't betrayed him. He hadn't seen him in over two decades and it was better to be safe than sorry.

"Ok. Where have you been? You say you've been tortured, I want to know everything. So spill it," said Alex.

"I was on an assignment undercover in Gilad's club. I don't know if they had some sort of intelligence on me but they somehow knew I wasn't who I said I was. I made my excuses to leave but her bodyguards chased and caught up with me. They attacked me so I fought them but they managed to knock me out and kidnap me. When I came round I was in a cell. A doctor called Revitska tortured me in some sort of operating theatre and wanted to know where Andra was. When I refuse to speak they exposed me to sunlight. When it took me a while to be affected they figured out that I was a firstborn. As I'm not one of the children of the blood with a little deduction they realised that I am your brother. At some point in the past they found out that by drinking blood from a vampire they can unlock withheld information. They get incredible boosts in strength and stamina but the consequences are fatal and there's no cure. Basically, if you're a vampire and you drink vampire blood you will die. Revitska and an ancient vampire called Saltorg forced some poor guy to drink from me. The only information he managed to give them was Roger and Sarah's address. I think they assumed it would be hours before he died. He burned like a fucking petrol bomb in less than a minute. It was horrible, I've never seen a vampire die with such a ferocious flame. Luckily he didn't have a chance to tell them about the base under the warehouse. I'm so sorry Alex. I never betrayed you, they took the information from me against my will. They used this curse against me. I hate being a vampire, I fucking hate it. I hate what I am. From then until this night they continued to torture me. They cut me to pieces until I wished that they had just fucking killed me, but they wouldn't let me die. They wanted information but I never told them a single thing. The pain was intolerable but I bore it. Days became months which in turn have become years. Time lost its meaning for me. All I knew was torture but still I bore the pain. I bore it so you wouldn't have to, so you would be safe and alive," said Vincent.

Tears rolled down his face as he spoke.

The stern look on Alex's face softened and he lowered the gun but kept it in his hand. In his heart he knew this was his brother and he found that he still trusted him. To him it wasn't like looking at a vampire, this was obviously his brother. He could see it in the way he moved and spoke. His mannerisms were that of a human, not something trying to appear human. He still felt the deep connection they had when they were young.

"How did you get here?" he said.

"When I wasn't being tortured I was kept in a tiny cell. They strapped me to a chair and force fed human blood. It has been the same every single night for all this time. Tonight, I heard fighting outside the cell, and then the door opened. A woman, a rogue vampire named Sapora, walked in and freed me. The vampires betrayed her so she's dedicated her life to killing them. We knew we would have to fight our way out but were outnumbered. Massively outnumbered. I did what I had to do to escape," said Vincent.

"What did you do? Where is this Sapora?" said Alex.

"We separated so I could get away. I did what I had to do to escape. I had no arms. There was no way we could have fought all those vampires," said Vincent.

"Vincent, what did you do?" said Alex.

"I...I bit three of them and drank their blood. It gave me back my arms and the strength to get out. It gave me the ability to find you," said Vincent.

"I thought you said vampire blood will kill you," said Alex.

"It will. I'm...I'm dying, Alex," said Vincent.

"No, you can't be. You've only just come back," said Alex.

He felt tears sting his eyes.

"I'm sorry, brother. I wouldn't have got out if I hadn't," said Vincent.

"We'll go to Andra. She will know something," said Alex.

"There is no cure, Alex. I'm running out of time," said Vincent.

"I'm not gonna just sit here and let you die!" said Alex.

"Alex, listen to me. Sapora told me that for you to complete the prophecy you must be bitten by a vampire," said Vincent.

"That's why they don't try to bite me?" said Alex.

"Yes. What vampire would sign the death sentence to their whole race, right? That is why I think I was born a vampire. I'm the only one who would do it. They have destroyed all our family and just about anyone we have ever loved. I want them to pay for what they have done," said Vincent.

Alex put the gun down on the floor and walked over to the sofa and stood infront of Vincent.

"I always knew there was something missing. I have been trained by Andra to fight and kill vampires for years. I never seemed to be fast enough to fight more than a few at a time. What do we need to do?"

Vincent stood up and looked at his twin. "I suppose I just need to bite you," he said.

"You suppose?" said Alex.

"I only found out about this tonight from a woman I never met before. She didn't give me a fucking manual," said Vincent.

"Ok, ok. Sorry I'm just I'm a little nervous," said Alex.

"Me too, lad. Me too. If I do this you know there is no turning back? I don't know what will happen to you but I'm guessing it's probably going to fucking hurt," said Vincent.

"This is what my whole life has been building up to. It's what I was born for," said Alex.

Vincent took hold of Alex in a hug and bared his teeth. He went to bite down then hesitated.

"There could be complications," he said.

"It's a risk I'm willing to take," said Alex.

He knew in his heart that this was the right thing to do but he still felt a bit scared.

'Isn't this how anyone would feel though? I have never felt fully human but this might turn me into something else. What happens if I lost myself in this thing? What if Alex no longer exists?' he thought to himself. He pushed the thoughts aside.

"The last time I saw you, you were a boy. Now you're a fully grown man. A hunter and killer of vampires. I'm so proud of you," said Vincent.

"I'm proud of you too, I knew you would never give up on me," said Alex.

Vincent smiled at his brother and then bared his teeth again. Alex felt his heartbeat quicken as Vincent took a breath and then bit down into his neck. His blood flowed into Vincent's mouth. It didn't taste sweet like human blood or bitter vampire blood, it tasted like sour like acid. His jaw spasmed and the glands in his mouth that held the vampiric saliva squeezed hard. Alex felt it being forced into his veins. Pain shot through Vincent's body, he pushed away from Alex and let out a scream of agony. He fell to the sofa but slid down to the floor.

Alex knelt down next to him as the wound in his neck pulsed with pain. Right now though he was more concerned about his brother.

"Vincent! Vincent! What's happening?" said Alex. Vincent looked up at his brother but his eyes stared wildly.

"It's happening Alex. I'm burning up. I'm dying," He threw his head back and screamed again as his flesh began to dry out and fissures appeared in his skin.

"What can I do?" said Alex with tears running down his face.

"Hold my head up brother. Let me look at you this last time," Vincent hissed through clenched teeth.
Alex lifted his brother's head. Vincent looked at him and smiled.

"Do you feel anything yet?" he said.

"My neck is getting hot and I can feel the heat spreading through my shoulder," said Alex.

"Let me see," said Vincent.
Alex moved his head to show Vincent his neck. Blood had run from the wound but it was already starting to congeal. The pain was becoming more intense but he had to bear it. Vincent needed him.

"It's happening Alex. Whatever happens promise me you will destroy them all. For me, for mum and dad, grandma and grandad, and for Scarlet," said Vincent.

"I promise, Vincent. I promise," said Alex.
Vincent clenched his teeth together as he stifled a scream but then opened his mouth and cried out. "I didn't think it would hurt this much."
His body shook and he tried to move his legs but they began to crumble as his body burnt from the inside. He

stared into Alex's eyes and tried to smile. A tear rolled down his cheek then soaked into his face as his skin began to turn grey. The fissures became cracks so deep his bones were visible. He coughed up droplets of blood but they fell out of the air as ash. With his last breathe he managed to say,

"I...love...you Alex."

"I love you too Vincent," said Alex. He was trying to be strong in his brother's last moments but his voice shuddered.

The words reached Vincent's ears just before died. His eyes rolled back in his head and his mouth fell open. His flesh smouldered with glowing embers and turned to ash. There were no flames and no explosion. Just embers and ashes where flesh had once been. Alex tried to hold his brother tighter but the body crumbled in his arms and fell apart. Alex sat and shook as he looked at the black grains that covered his hands. Tears rolled down his face and for a moment he made no noise at all, then slowly a cry rose out of him. A wail that embodied all his anguish that had built up over the years and he sobbed over the ashes of his twin. He cried for his mum and dad, his grandma and grandad, and now his brother too. He cried because with the death of Vincent he was alone in the world. The last member of his family.

Anger boiled in his veins and he promised himself that every vampire would perish. Every single one of them. Ruhsarr would pay for what he had done to the Austin family. He would pay for what he had done to the world.

A pain grew in his chest. It was not just emotion, it was real. He clutched at his chest as the pain shot down into his legs then up into his head. As it did there was a bang at the door. His skin started to tingle. Something slammed against the door. The locks held but the door buckled inwards. He managed to haul himself to his feet despite the pain that ravaged his body. The thing slammed against the door again. His feet were like lead as he stumbled across the living room in an attempt to reach one of the UV light switches. Before he could get to it the door burst open and four vampires ran in. One of them swung a battering ram at his hip like Charlie Chaplin's umbrella. He moved his huge and muscled frame through the room. As he did he looked around the room, then at Alex, and smiled.

"Alex Austin I presume?" he said with an American accent." Shit, you and Vincent were identical, huh? We won't need any kind of test to determine if you were related. You look exactly like him, except for the hair. Tell me…Where is he?" said the vampire.

Alex continued to stumble towards the switch.

"Look, Tank. That must be what's left of him," said the woman of the group in a German accent as she pointed at the pile of ash on the floor.

Alex let out a groan as tears ran down his face and he was sweating profusely.

"Aww, look at him. He's crying," said the woman. She ran over and kicked Alex down to the floor. He lay there on his side. He had been only another two steps from the switch.

"Are you sad little man? Is your brother dead? Oh, boohoo," she taunted and kicked him in the stomach.

"Your cold, Blanc," Tank said to her with a grin. They all laughed as they stood over Alex.

"Some prophesised hero you turned out to be. You're

crying so much you can't even fight," said Tank.

All four of them kicked and stamped on him repeatedly as his body began to convulse. Debilitating pain kept him curled up on the floor and a burning sensation swept over his skin. He held his arms across his abdomen as his internal organs felt like they were being twisted and stretched.

A tall thin member of the group reached down and lifted Alex up by the throat.

"We're gonna kill you nice and slow. You're going to wish you had died along with your mother," he said in a Russian accent.

"Raven, what's that on his neck? Oh shit. Is that a fucking bite?" said the shortest, sinewy member of the group and he took a step back.

"No, shut up, Blur. That's not a bite. We must have cut him when we were beating him," said Blanc.
Alex looked at them and forced a smile despite all the pain.

"Yes… it's… a bite. Vincent got to me…. before you could. You're all… fucking dead," he said.
He had to force the words out between his blood soaked teeth in his clenched jaws. He looked Raven in the eye.
"You're gonna wish… I had died… you cunt," he growled.
Raven threw him down to the floor then stamped his foot down onto Alex's head, slamming it against the laminate with a heavy thud. Alex let out a long scream that dropped three octaves in pitch. His body began to writhe and his limbs contorted in strange angles.

"Oh fuck. Oh fuck!" said Blur as he ran his fingers through his thick blue hair then held his head in his hands.

"It's ok. It's…ok. This doesn't change anything. We can still kill him before he changes," said Tank

"Fucking no, Tank. It's not ok. It's not ok at all. We're fucked, man. We're all fucked!" said Blur as he backed away from Alex.

"Blur, come back here. It's ok. We can do this!" said Tank.

But Blur, like his name suggested, was gone. Tank looked too the other two vampires.

"We got to kill him and fast. If he changes, well, you can cancel any plans you have for tomorrow," he said. Blanc pulled out a long thin dagger and stabbed Alex repeatedly in the back. Raven stamped on his head and Tank brought the battering ram down repeatedly onto his shoulders. Alex writhed and twisted as blood poured from his wounds. His bones cracked as they shifted and grew under his flesh. His muscles convulsed and pulled his limbs into strange and horrifying positions. The burning sensation in his skin was so intense he may as well have been on fire. He screamed so hard he thought his throat would explode. Pain shot through his head as the bones of his skull and face split apart and changed shape.

The vampires were so busy trying to kill him, they didn't notice he was getting bigger. Alex's vocal cords stopped making any noise. He got onto his hands and knees and curled up into a ball. Still, they kept on beating him. His shirt split up the back as his chest expanded. His skin thickened and turned grey. Blanc's knife no longer punctured his flesh, so she pulled out a gun and shot him four times. The bullets bounced off without leaving a mark. Alex shot out his hands and grabbed Raven by the knees.

"Get him off me! Get him off! He's crushing my knees!" he screamed.

Tank and Blanc attacked Alex as violently as they possibly could but nothing they did had any effect.

Alex threw his arms open so wide and with such force that Raven was torn open from crotch to sternum. His organs splattered in a bloody mess upon the floor and he screamed once before he and his viscera burned up.

Tank and Blanc cried out in shock and recoiled in revulsion and horror. Alex stood up and looked at his attackers who were both now much shorter than him. Blanc lunged at him, pointing her knife at his heart. He caught her by the wrist and lifted her off the ground. She dangled in front of him in the way a rabbit would be held up by its ears by a hunter.

"Let go of me you fucking fucker," she screamed as her bones cracked.

He watched her for a second, bemused as she fruitlessly lashed out at him with her other hand. He hit her in the chest with his open palm. There was a rip of flesh and she flew across the room. She slammed into the wall with such force that her body left an imprint in the brickwork. She then slid to the floor and lay motionless. Her right arm was still gripped in Alex's huge hand.

Tank stood watching and shook with fear as Alex's head shifted and changed shape. His jaws grew in length forcing his nose to become a snout. He then opened his mouth and roared. His teeth sank into his gums and new, long, serrated teeth pushed up to take their place. Instinct then kicked in and Tank ran for the door using all his vampiric speed. But before he even got out into the hall Alex grabbed him by the shoulders and dragged him back into the room. Something happened then that no one could have ever expected. Before he could stop himself and for reasons he did not yet understand Alex took a huge bite out of the vampire's neck and swallowed it whole. Tank opened his mouth to scream but no sound came and he just stood motionless except for an almost imperceptible shudder. He looked like he was going to burn up but his flesh hardened outwards from the wound and became like grey porcelain. Something inside Alex drove him to bite more chunks from this husk and he devoured them. Soon Tank was gone.

A pulse of energy ran through Alex like an electric shock as he ate. He quivered and flexed his shoulders as his muscle mass increased as his limbs continued to grow.

Blanc moaned from across the room and raised her head. She saw this huge beast flick its head back and crunch down the last morsels of something. Raven's ashes still lay on the floor but Tank was nowhere to be seen. She opened her mouth and wailed. She tried to stop it and clamped her hand to her mouth but the thing had already heard her. It turned and looked at her. It was like nothing she had ever seen. Humanoid but massive and its long lizard-like head was still changing shape. It looked right at her and its eyes shone silver. It worked its jaws and pulled the shredded remains of one of Tank's boots from between its teeth. It took a step towards her, she put her hand out infront of her and screamed. In four strides it reached her, dragged her from the floor, and bit into her shoulder. Her body twitched as the blood in her veins ground to a halt. The world went dull as her eyes hardened and her body solidified.

Alex tore into her remains until he reached her waist. He threw out his arms. The burning sensation in his flesh reached its peak as thick dark grey scales burst out from his skin over every inch of his body. They then flattened down and hardened into a reptilian armour.

Chapter 39.

When the vampires had smashed open the door to
Alex's flat an alarm began to wail in the S.O.V.E.U.
Base 107 control room. The soldier on duty looked at the
light set into the control panel on the desk. It was
labelled 'Alex's apartment' and flashed in time with the
alarm. He pressed the intercom button to Andra's
quarters.

"Ma'am. This is control. We have a situation," he said.
Andra was lay in bed. She rarely slept but at times found
it beneficial to rest and relax. However, this was not
going to be one of those times. She climbed out of bed
and ran to the intercom on her desk and pressed the
button.

"This is Andra. Go ahead control," she said.

"We have an alarm triggered at Alex's apartment,"
said the soldier.

"Thank you control, I'll handle it from here," she
switched the intercom to tannoy. "This is Lieutenant
Colonel Hudson. I want my attack team ready and in the
garage in five minutes. You hear me? Davis, Hughes,
Hussain, Mc'Ready, Palmer, and White. I want you
suited and booted and in the garage in five. Alex is in
trouble and we need to be there before the authorities."

There was a flurry of activity in the personnel
dormitory as the soldiers got dressed into their uniforms
and body armour and collected their equipment. Andra
stood in the garage as the team assembled. They saluted
her, she returned the gesture, and ushered them into a
waiting van. With White in the driving seat, they sped
out of the garage, up past the security measures, and out

of the warehouse. Andra then ran them through her plan.

"Alex's apartment has been breached. It may be nothing but we have to suspect a vampire attack so listen up. We'll enter the property via the south staircase. We go quick and quiet. Once we're in we'll assess the situation and react accordingly. Attach your suppressers. I don't want this to turn into a firefight but if it does I don't want the whole police force on our back. Any question?" she said.

"No Ma'am," said the team in unison.

"Ok, be ready. ETA two minutes," said White. The apartment was only about a mile away and at this time on a Saturday morning there was hardly any traffic. As they drove they loaded their weapons and made some final equipment and ammunition checks.

They reached the apartments and the van screeched to a halt as close to the entrance as possible. Andra stepped out of the van and as she did she saw Blur run away from the building. She quickly raised her gun and shot him in the shins. He staggered slightly before he fell to the ground and flipped head over heels. The soldiers ran over and held him down.

"Let me go. We're all fucked. It's all over!" said Blur.

"What the fuck are you talking about?" said Hughes.

"He's been bitten. He's gonna kill us all," said Blur.

"Is he talking about Alex?" said Palmer.

"I think so," said Andra.

"You're not Vampires are you?" said Blur.

"No, we're not. We're the S.O.V.E.U." said Andra.

"Oh fuck! Help! Help me!" cried Blur.

"Shut up," said Hussain.

"Help!" pleaded Blur.

With one swift movement Hussain pushed the barrel of her MP5 between his teeth.

"You're just another dead vampire to me, man," said Hussain and place her finger on the trigger.

Blur's screams died in his throat.

"Hussain, stand down! I want him alive," said Andra just in time.

Hussain lifted her finger from the trigger and flicked on the safety.

"Don't even think about moving," she said as she glared into Blurr's eyes.

"Hughes and Palmer, chain him up and put him in the back of the van. The rest of you with me," said Andra.

Hussain stepped away. Hughes flipped Blur over and rammed his face against the floor as Palmer chained his wrist to his ankles. They dragged him back to the vehicle and threw him inside.

"Looks like you get to see another day, Chuckle fuck," said Hughes as he slammed the door.

The quiet of the night was broken by four gunshots.

"We have to get in there on the double," said Andra. She and the soldiers ran into the entrance of the apartment block but the lift was on the top floor.

"We're wasting time, I'm taking point," said Andra and began to run up the stairs. They made quick and quiet progress with Hussain, White, Mc'Ready, and Davis in the middle, Hughes, and Palmer following behind. They could hear the screams and the sounds of fighting as they reached the fifth floor.

"Ok. Be ready," whispered Andra.

White opened the door and the rest of them moved into the hallway. There were six apartments per floor. Alex's apartment was easily identifiable by the destroyed door. Andra ran in first in the usual plan but was stopped in her tracks by what she saw. She stood motionless and staring as the others ran in behind her. They stopped too, they all raised their guns and aimed at the thing in the room. Its huge mass was crouched down as it gnawed on what looked like the remains of a human. There was no blood at all and the innards looked like mummified flesh.

"Hold your fire," whispered Andra.

"What the fuck is that thing?" said Mc'Ready and shifted uneasily.

Her finger squeezed the trigger of her Diemaco C7A2.

"Mc'Ready, hold your fire," said Andra.

The thing looked over at them as its attention was drawn away from its meal. Its flesh was dark grey and the texture of crocodile skin. Its silver eyes scanned them all one by one. Small chunks of dried flesh hung between the teeth of its elongated jaws. Its eyes stopped on Mc'Ready and she shifted again. It let out a deep rumbling growl that was almost too low to hear and vibrated through the air.

"Mc'Ready," said Andra in a strained whisper.

"Ma'am, what the fuck is this thing?" said Hughes. The soldiers all twitched nervously. Moving their arms and readjusting their stances.

"I said hold your fucking fire!" said Andra.

The thing stood up to its full nine feet and roared at them. The sound it made was so loud it made the walls of the room shake. They all stepped back from its huge mass. The muscles in its body flexed as it displayed its enormous potential strength. Plates of scales ran down its arms, legs, and back. Its head was massive with a long lizard-like snout and two long nostrils on either side. Its jaws were heavily muscled and full of what looked like venom glands.

"Ma'am?" said Hussain.

"I said hold your fucking fire!" said Andra.

Andra looked into its eyes. What she saw seemed not like anger but frustration.

"Alex. Is that you?" she said.

The beast stopped roaring and relaxed out of its aggressive stance.

"Alex, it's ok. We won't shoot you. Come with us, we can help you," said Andra.

His lips drew back from his teeth, he shook his head and let out a grunt of disapproval. He then turned his head and looked over at the window.

"No, Alex, come with us, please," said Andra, trying to appeal to whatever was left of Alex within this beast. He looked back at her for a moment, but then turned and ran at the window. He crashed through it and took most of the wall with him. Andra ran over to the hole he had made and looked down. The wind whipped her hair around her face as she watched the beast fall the six storeys to the ground below. He landed on his feet in the carpark. The impact shattered the concrete, broke windows and set off car alarms. He looked back up at Andra, then turned away and ran into the darkness of the night.

To be continued...

Author bio

Paul J. Kearns is an author from Bolton, Northwest England. He lives there with his wife and two children.

From a young age Paul has had an interest in writing. He is also a fan of all things dark and horrifying.

After leaving school he started working as a dental technician and earned a B-Tec National diploma and a UCHE in Dental Technology from the Manchester Metropolitan University. He still works as a Dental Technician today.

In his spare time he loves to spend time with his family and besides writing, he likes watching movies, gaming, and drawing.

He started writing this novel series in 2010. Before that, he had written a few short stories but had no experience in the art of novel writing. So what you hold in your hands is over 12 years of learning and honing the skills needed.

Dear reader,

I hope you enjoyed reading this book. I hope you enjoyed the story, and love them or hate them I hope you were drawn in by the characters.

If you were inspired in any way to write that story you have been thinking of, I would encourage you to go ahead with it.

And remember, don't be afraid of the dark, be afraid of the things that use it as camouflage.

Printed in Great Britain
by Amazon

77160621R00159